Ma

Also by James Albany
in Pan Books

Warrior Caste
Mailed Fist
Deacon's Dagger
Close Combat

James Albany

Marching Fire

Pan Original
Pan Books London and Sydney

First published 1983 by Pan Books Ltd, Cavaye Place, London SW10 9PG

ISBN 0 330 28033 3
Printed and bound in Great Britain by
Richard Clay (The Chaucer Press) Ltd, Bungay, Suffolk

The gathering of information in the Malay States was an odd business. My former Scotland Yard colleagues would have blanched at the tricks I had to get up to in order to bring terrorists to justice. While I have nothing but praise for the support I received from army units it is my belief that the work of 'narks' and 'squealers' removed more names from the Wanted List than all the jungle patrols. In the Spring of 1952 I was summoned urgently to the Port Kernan Police District on the West Coast of Perak. Here the guerrillas were so firmly entrenched in the local community that they operated with near impunity and might have continued to do so if I had not arrived in the nick of time from 'Head Office' in Singapore. The resident squadron of the Special Air Service had received a crushing blow. It was up to me to penetrate the wall of fear and the conspiracy of silence among the Chinese population and to root out the villain who was behind the sneak attacks. He was a Communist Chinese well known in Perak and other Northern States. His name was Wei Sand Shan. In my view Shan's reputation as a jungle fighter had been exaggerated. I decided to devote myself to uncovering and cutting off Shan's channels of Supply and Intelligence, a decision which I was not to regret, although it almost cost me my life.

Colonel A. K. Saunders
Jungle Copper

********* *S.A.S.*
COMBAT MANUAL

The Ambushing of Insurgents

Section 1 – Policy
General

1. A higher proportion of insurgent eliminations are achieved by ambushes with better opportunity for kills than any other form of contact. Particularly when chances of contacts are remote, it is essential to take full advantage of every chance offered. Ambushes laid as the result of direct high grade information must be based on sound and detailed planning with execution by specially selected troops.

*

4. To fully exploit the information received from SB agents, it is essential to choose the best possible team to make the contact. This may frequently entail a company commander leading an ambush group, although it may consist of only a handful of men. Men especially selected for their marksmanship or other particular qualities should be drawn from any element of the unit and, in fact, the ambush group may consist of men from different services. The overriding consideration in selecting the ambush party is to choose the team most likely to succeed . . .

Contents

Up country

Sergeant Buz Campbell, a burly Canadian, opened one gummy eyelid and surveyed the sky. In fact, he could see precious little of the clear, washed-blue cover, for gigantic *gelam* swamp-trees flung their ragged umbrella leaves overhead. He didn't feel good. For all sorts of reasons he felt lousy. At least the sting had gone out of the tail of the spring sumatra though big droplets still plopped from the vegetation and the bark of the tree against which Campbell hung stank like a latrine brush.

He opened the other eye.

'Hey, wee man?'

There was no response.

'You there, P.B.?' said Buz without moving.

'Aye, where the hell else would I be?'

'Tell you somethin'.'

'What?'

'A secret.'

'What?'

'It's stopped rainin'.'

'So it has.'

'That's not the secret.'

'What, well?'

Buz sighed. The hammock rocked gently from side to side. Its steel clip-hook squeaked against the wet branch to which it was attached, tightening the grip of rot-proof nylon rope around Buz Campbell's boots.

'P.B.?'

'Aye.'

'Know what?'

'What?'

'I'm forty-five years old.'

'Is that all?'

'Today.'

Silence, then the Scot's voice croaked, without much enthusiasm, *'Happy Birthday t'you, Happy Birthday t'you. Happy Birthdaaay, Buz Caaampbell, Haaa—'*

'Keep it down,' Deacon snapped.

Captain Jeffrey Alexander Deacon had just extricated himself from his sleeping net and was seated on it as on a swing. His pale, spidery legs dangled five feet above the suppurating green surface of the swamp. He had washed his mouth out with neat gin and dabbed the alcohol gently on to several angry-looking tick bites on his thighs. He took another swig from the canteen. He did not spit the Gordon's out this time but swallowed it. Major Beasley, OC 'K' Squadron, SAS, would have had a purple fit at this form of ablution.

'I will personally file court martial papers on any man under my command who fills his canteen with a spiritous beverage,' the Beezer would bellow. 'I will not tolerate such flagrant abuse of the privileges accorded to the men of my Squadron. Self-sufficiency may be – I say '*may* be' – a much-vaunted virtue in the short history of Special Air Service regiments, but privilege does *not* extend – I say '*not* extend' – to behaving like a bunch of drunken louts while on duty. When you are on patrol, every minute of every hour of every day, I consider you to be as much on duty as if you were standing at arms in front of the guard house. Do I make myself clear?'

Yes, sir. Yes, sir. Clear as a bell, sir.

Too bloody clear, sir.

The Beezer was not all mouth. He was an excellent CO in many respects and an administrator without equal. But he did rattle on. Besides, the Beezer had never been in the hinterland of Malaya, had never endured twenty-nine consecutive days and nights lurking in the sort of country God must have tossed away after He finished the Creation. If the SAS expected you to live on handfuls of oatmeal, tinned bully and tea, plus what you could scrounge from the swamp, then the SAS could not expect you to behave like a bloody Boy Scout.

Deacon slid his backside from the hammock and lowered himself gingerly into the scummy water which lay beneath the *gelam* tree. P.B. was still hanging from an upper branch. A mosquito net of parachute silk was wrapped around his hammock like the cocoon of an overblown moth. Buz, however, had shed the silk. The captain waded through the shallow swamp and offered the canteen to the sergeant.

'Good morning, Birthday Boy,' Deacon said. 'Have one on the house. A small one, though.'

'Forty-goddamned-five,' Buz growled despondently. 'God, Deke, suddenly, I'm an old man.'

'True,' said Deacon. 'Time you were put to pasture, Buz. I'll bring the matter to Major Beasley's notice as soon as we return.'

'I mean, Jesus, I'm *really* forty-five,' said Buz.

'What does it say on your documents?' Deacon asked.

'Thirty-eight.'

'A man's only as old as his service record, you know. Do you want a snifter, Buz, or not?'

'Sure.'

Buz hauled himself out of the snare of the hammock and into a contorted position with arm, shoulder and head free of the ropes. He took the canteen, tilted it and swallowed a large mouthful of watered gin. In sweat-stained undervest, unshaven and ungroomed, his eyes red with fatigue and his skin blotched with insect bites, Buz would not have passed the morning muster with Major Beasley. He *did* look his age, looked twice his age, in fact.

'Friggin' gin,' Buz growled. 'Don't know how you can stand that piss, Deke.'

''Cause he's English,' said P.B., whose stock of Scotch had run out four days ago. 'Hey, Buz, bet you never thought you'd be spendin' your forty-fifth birthday hangin' from a tree in Malaya, eh?'

'Right.'

'Wonder where you'll be when you're fifty.'

'Dead'n' bloody buried.'

'Never!' said Deacon. 'You'll be living a life of luxury and ease on a sunny beach in California.'

'On an army pension?' said Buz. 'Anyhow, I can't stand California.'

P.B. McNair unwrapped himself from his cocoon and descended into the foot of water which passed for solid ground in the Totan swamp country. He had been lured from repose by the promise of alcohol. Generously, Deacon handed over the canteen to the little Scot. Captain and corporal leaned against the bole of the tree, feet on the gnarled roots which crouched above the water level. Weapons and gear were stored in the tree's capacious niches to keep them dry. The food supply, what was left of it, dangled in a large Bergen rucksack from a branch where, in theory, rats, ants and monkeys couldn't get at it. Discipline was all to the men of 'K' Squadron. P.B. rationed himself to one mouthful from the metal canteen. He capped it and returned it to Deacon then, leaning on the sergeant's shoulder, grinned and said, 'In five years, Buz, my guess is you'll still be swannin' round this fuckin' swamp.'

'Skip it, wee man. I ain't in the mood for discussin' my future at this goddamned hour of the day.'

'You'll never let her go, Buz.'

Abruptly the sergeant rolled out of the hammock. He dropped expertly to the watery ground. He hauled down his blanket and the mosquito net and draped them over a bough to dry out, should the sun happen to shine long enough.

'How do I know what the frig I'm gonna do?' Buz grumbled. 'I'm happy just to get through 'til nightfall.'

'But the lassie—'

'Shoot to it, Corporal,' Buz barked. 'Rustle up breakfast, right?'

'Right.'

Arriving at the age of maturity hadn't helped Buz Campbell's temper. Long separations from his woman in Port Kernan had altered his outlook on life. He was no less efficient as a fighting soldier but his enthusiasm for deep probe operations which carried him far into the wilderness and away from Susu for weeks on end had dwindled to minus zero. Deacon, P.B. and big Buz Campbell's other friends understood it. It wasn't just that he missed the kid's loving; he was scared she would find another guy, a younger guy, while he was up country.

Susu had drifted into Port Kernan, into Buz Campbell's ken, along with other ambassadors of sin and civilisation, in the wake of the establishment of an army garrison on the outskirts of the town. Though Campbell called her 'his lady', he knew goddamned well what she was, a hustling kid who had seen more of the seamy side of life than he had, near enough, and who would have wound up as a 'B' girl if he hadn't taken up with her. Susu was seventeen years old, sweet-faced and seemingly innocent. Christ, he was probably ten years older than her goddamned mother.

Sensing Buz's mood, Deacon and P.B. avoided conversation and got on with the morning's chores.

P.B. fished down the ration sack and measured parched oatmeal into a clean tin can. He burrowed into the roots of the biggest of the trees on the island of semi-dry ground on which the soldiers were camped, found the cooking stove in its tin box. He lit a paraffin brick and set the can on top of it, filled a larger tin with water which he had collected from the pools among the tree roots and which he had doctored already with a couple of purifying pills. He stood it ready to put on the burner when the oatmeal was warm. He unwrapped the strip of dried fish which Deacon had bought from a native village six days ago. The fish looked like a chunk of black driftwood and it came off the bones like pencil shavings. But it flavoured the porridge a wee bit and gave them something to stick in their teeth. It was a bloody sight better than another slice of ham-and-egg pudding out of a green tin.

The eager young punters who roared to join the SAS or the Royal Marine Commando might have been less keen if they'd known how bloody boring the real work of soldiering could be 'up there' on the pointed tip of the huge military and police organisation which was dedicated to eliminating the Communist Menace from Malaya. Show them an 'average' breakfast, let them live up to their ballocks in fungus and frog-water for a week and maybe you'd get home to them what the reality was like. Even then there'd be some, many, who would trek a thousand miles for the chance to prove themselves. Proving anything much was beyond the five-man group which had pushed across one hundred and thirty miles of the remotest mush this side of the Thai border. Even Jeffrey Alexander Deacon had almost lost his keenness for the hunt, his desire for vengeance against the communist guerrilla leader, Wei Sand Shan.

Laboriously, P.B. made breakfast. It would be the only meal eaten in daylight hours. They wouldn't have another cook-up until dusk and would peg along on 'snacks' of fruit – if they could find any – or gnaw sticks of the black fish; whatever they could scrounge from the swamp, excluding grubs and snakes, since that was one SAS 'myth' which had but a slender basis in fact, at least among the men of 'K' Squadron.

While the corporal was thus engaged, Deacon leaned on the hammock and extracted a notebook from its oilskin wallet. Within the notebook were folded four little maps neatly penned on rice-paper. The captain handled them as reverently as if they were holy relics. The maps had been compiled from information 'yielded up' by two lowly terrorists who had been flushed out of a *kampong* near the river crossing at Tengatok five weeks ago. They had begged to be allowed to surrender their arms, being – they declared – heartily sick of Wei Sand Shan's demands and the life of an insurgent in the guerrilla army. Deacon didn't trust the young men. Nobody did. But RAF dare-devil flyers had obligingly flown a couple of photo reconnaissance missions over the area and details seemed to tally.

The Totan swamp was definitely 'up country'. Foot patrols had not been far into the region and aborigines from its tiny, primitive communities were difficult to pin down. It remained an almost unknown patch, just the sort of location in which Wei Sand Shan might choose to lie low for a while, build up his reserves of men and weapons. A thready river, the Sungai Konyang, seeped from the swamp's north-eastern edge and nudged along the foothills of the Bukit Basar. According to the pair of 'heroes' now undergoing rehabilitation Wei Sand Shan had a big camp on the river, though they had not personally been to the spot. The camp was supplied by canoe and raft but once every month a pack-train of bullock-carts and bearers came in from Kelantan.

The fact that Shan's 'camp' did not show on aerial photographs meant nothing. Jungle cover was too effective for penetration and Shan would have no problem in keeping the camp hidden. The monthly pack-train was a better angle to work on.

The prisoners, though, could yield no high-grade information on its source. Intelligence and Special Branch agents had long been aware that Shan had a Chinese fat-cat behind him. But investigation had provided no clues as to who the 'money-shark' might be. Shan was no longer officially connected with the Malayan Communist Party. He would have no truck with the Min Yuen, the Communist underground. He was respected by MCP officials as the most cunning and daring of all rebel leaders, but was held in bad odour by the political wing. It was obvious that Shan had an independent organisation which functioned undetected under the Security Forces' noses.

Major Tim Dalinart had discussed the matter with Deacon.

'What do we do?' he asked.

'Send in a spear,' Deacon promptly answered.

'From which side of the hill? By river, do you think?'

'Truck to the Australian Plantation and hike to the swamp.'

'Not the river?'

'Shan can defend the river,' Deacon said. 'Besides, by the sound of it what's going up the river isn't much more than the morning milk and newspapers. No, I'm absolutely sure that what we want to latch on to is the monthly supply train.'

'But we haven't a clue as to its route. Our informants claim they don't know.'

'Geographical deductive reasoning, Timothy. Bullock-carts can't cross proper swamp. Let's check our geological survey maps for rock ridges.'

'It might be weeks before the train comes through.'

'So?'

'Big medicine, Deacon. A long spear is expensive.'

'For the destruction of a terrorist training camp and arms depot it would surely be worth the effort.'

'Completely,' Tim Dalinart had said. 'But it's Shan you're after, isn't it, old chap?'

'Absolutely,' Deacon had admitted. 'He got away from me once but he won't escape again. Not if I have to drive a stake through his horrid little heart.'

'How will we string the chain?'

'Three radios from a jungle base not too far from the Australian,' said Deacon. 'A five-man team out on the tip.'

'You?'

'If you think me fit for it?'

'Even the Beezer won't baulk at putting the local legend to the fore. Will you have a radio?'

'I think not. I'd prefer to keep weight to a minimum. Besides, we can arrange a runner between the forward team and the next link. I'd be obliged, however, if you'd ensure that we have a radio expert with each of the three back-up units.'

'Done,' Dalinart had said.

'Once we spot the supply train—'

'*If* you spot the supply train.'

'—we'll track it to the camp and send a runner back to the nearest radio team who will, of course, be stationary not mobile. Quick flash down the line will summon a bomb drop on the exact location of the camp.'

'How will you mark the camp?'

'Fire and smoke,' said Deacon.

'What if Shan has a large force of men there?'

'We'll crawl off and await the arrival of groups two and three before we attack.'

'Promise?'

'Absolutely.'

'It *would* be rather nice to nail the fat-cat too.'

'That's asking a bit much. Anyhow, it isn't really our department. Special Branch should get something good out of the raid, however.'

'Jeffrey, your confidence overwhelms me.'

After twenty-nine days in the heart of the Totan swamp country, however, Deacon's confidence had waned.

He was beginning to wonder if the Chinese fugitives had been planted by Shan to create diversion for the SAS and other outfits involved in 'Operation Bogwater', as the Beezer had unimaginatively named it. At this moment Shan might be sitting at ease three hundred miles away, chortling up his sleeve – except that Shan was a sober little butcher-boy and did not 'chortle' at anything.

With so much rain over the Totan, it was impossible to read tracks. Deacon and his team had combed the long 'ridge' along the edge of the swamp to no avail. There had been no sightings of any kind, not even of aborigines. The team's Dyak tracker claimed to know where villages were and suggested that the natives should be questioned. Innocent as the natives seemed to be, Deacon could not quite bring himself to trust them. He preferred to steer clear. He was conscious of the fact that they were sitting ducks should Shan's guerrillas catch them by surprise. One of the penalties of working small units deep into the forest was that after a while you could not be sure who was stalking who.

Umgah, the Dyak tracker, and Gurkha Sergeant Johnny Badhur had taken the 'dawn patrol'. They were stationed a couple of miles to the north-east in a bowl of boulders and snake-thorn which lay on the slope above the 'ridge'. The ridge was nothing more than a shading on the geological maps of the region, which showed firm ground. Vegetation was marginally different from that of the surrounding swamp. Beyond it lay another elbow of swamp land which cocked to the base of Bukit Basar, a series of hills of no great height or prominence.

Deacon had been tempted to worm up into the Bukit Basar using the ridge as a line finder. But the frail chain of communication with the units stationed behind them depended upon his maintaining a 'post' here. Not until the supply train or a positive movement of CTs had been sighted would Deacon risk pushing forward into the Bukit Basar, and only after

Johnny and P.B. had been sent to carry word back to the nearest of the radio units.

One facet of the operation gave Deacon hope of success, the fact that they had seen no living human being in their twenty-day watch. If he had a camp in the area, Shan would have put out sentries rather than patrols, and the aboriginal tribes would have herded their goats, gathered their chickens and drifted passively away out of range of the guerrillas. The jungle jealously guarded such secrets. Deacon had no option but to sit it out. Though none of them was showing signs of sickness or disease, they were exhausted by the oppressive swamp country and its steamy rain. Even the Dyak. And when a chap born and bred in North Borneo lost his bounce, you took heed of the signs that the *tuans* must be running close to break point.

As if reading the captain's mind, Buz Campbell asked, 'How long we gonna stay here, Deke?'

'Another forty-eight hours.'

'What if they don't show?'

'We'll pull back as far as Kuala Dipang and rest up.'

'Then come back?'

'How do you feel about it?'

'Lousy.'

'I understand.'

'I ain't no kid, Jeff. I'm forty-five years old. Anyhow, might be another twenty days before the train comes through. We ain't vittled for that kind of stay.'

'We'll pull out to Kuala Dipang and radio for a relief platoon to push through to the point.'

'And what if we miss 'em during the change-over?'

'Buz, for God's sake!'

'Yeah. Sorry.'

Deacon too was disheartened. It had been almost a year since last he'd had a chance to wound Sand Shan's organisation. After the wide-open combat at the Wade-Wingfield rubber plantation, the guerrilla leader had shown himself much less willing to engage in direct confrontation with the SAS.

Shan had staged a dozen lightning attacks against important

targets across the state and, in every case, had been successful. The North Point Mining Company's site at Turong had been badly damaged, three white engineers killed. The Catholic Medical Mission at Sungai Kangor had been subjected to two vicious night raids, resulting in the deaths of eleven nurses and two doctors, in addition to Malay patients. A subtle ambush had been laid for a platoon of the Pioneers near Port Kernan itself, with a tally of seven dead and nineteen wounded.

In all of these guerrilla-style assaults Sand Shan's planning had been thorough and he had sacrificed few men. So far as the Intelligence Branch could ascertain, however, Shan had not led the raids in person. He had delegated responsibility to his henchman, Kwai Yan Chung, a mountainous rebel from the Hokkien Province of China who had been imported by Shan as his second-in-command. Yan Chung's name appeared just below that of Wei Sand Shan on Special Branch's 'Most Wanted' list.

Breakfast over, the SAS men 'closed up' camp. Provision sacks, hammocks and nets were carefully hidden in the upper branches of the trees. In an hour or less Johnny Badhur and the Dyak would return here to rest and would have to ferret out the gear once more. But Deacon took no chances. The last thing he wanted was to tip their presence in the area to Sand Shan. Carrying their weapons, the three soldiers quit the shelter of the *gelam* thicket and headed across the still, shallow swamp.

Landmarks had become monotonously familiar – a gnarled root, a spray of flowering vines, a spiny palm standing alone like a sentinel. The route covered a half-mile through sour water and another mile through fern and undergrowth. Deacon thrust forward, nudging the scummy surface with an odd shuffle step which made very little noise and was not too tiring. Spaced at ten-yard intervals, P.B. and Buz followed.

Dappled with sunlight, trees stood motionless as far as the eye could see. The air was thick and humid. The men sweated heavily. Clouds of insects plagued them constantly. Small wonder Shan's encampment had not been rumbled, tucked away in the midst of such frightful wilderness, far from paddis and *kampongs* where food could be extorted from the villagers and fruit holdings raided with comparative ease.

Deacon was curious as to how Shan kept his soldiers happy in this hell-hole, how he kept their spirits alive to the ideals of Communism. The answer lay in the mysterious monthly ox-cart train which ground its way out of nowhere through the festering jungle, laden with goodies for guerrillas-in-training. If Deacon's guess was correct then the monthly 'delivery' was the life-line and life-blood of the CT encampment, vital to Shan's power and long-term intentions.

Deacon signalled to P.B. who in turn signalled to Buz Campbell. All three stooped into the stalks of the gigantic ferns which, laced with tough grass of the *lalang* variety, crowded under the tall trees.

Moving like a monkey, P.B. came up to the captain.

'What's wrong, Deke?' he whispered.

'I hear something.'

P.B. listened. 'Aye.'

'What?'

'It's no' a burd.'

Concentration made the hum of the insect cloud seem as loud as a dynamo. But there wasn't much else to distract the ears of the SAS men.

Buz Campbell joined his colleagues. 'You hear it too?'

'Plane?' said P.B.

Buz shook his head. 'Somethin' slower. It's comin' this way.'

Deacon grinned. 'Perhaps we're going to be in luck after all.'

They spoke like three men sharing a single match, heads together under the spore-laden leaves of the ferns.

'How far to the meet?' asked Buz.

'Quarter of a mile, north.'

Cautiously, Buz got to his feet and stretched himself to his full height. He canted his head this way and that. 'Gone,' he murmured. 'Hey, no. There we go again, folks.'

'Let's push on at the double,' said Deacon. 'We'd best link with Johnny and the Dyak. We'll require legs if it *is* the supply column.'

'Aye, but we'll need an eyeball first,' said P.B. 'Canny just go clumpin' back t' the radio op. with a vague report.'

'I agree absolutely,' said Deacon.

Hastening now, the SAS men made their way through the undergrowth. Soon the ferns thinned and the *lalang* thickened into a broad beige patch, chest-high. There were stones and little grey flints among the roots, subtle indications that the footing was firm. It was along a line adjacent to this grassland that the track ran, just above it that Johnny and Umgah were hidden.

Scouting first, Deacon raised his right arm. A pause; then came an answering signal, an unmistakable, low *chucking* like an apprehensive pheasant, an imitation which the Dyak did perfectly.

Deacon, P.B. and Buz came out of the grass patch and through thin underbrush into fern again. There was no impediment here; this was the track. Umgah had turned up its line without difficulty, finding animal droppings and, in spite of the rain, the faint impress of broad wooden wheels which were common to native produce carts.

The Gurkha was on his belly, Enfield service rifle trained, while Umgah, in crotch-cloth and tennis shoes, squatted behind the trunk of a sapling, a short spear in his left hand and a *parang*, a long-handled cleaver, in his right.

Over months of patrolling, Deacon had grown accustomed to the sight of the Dyak. To 'new recruits' who teamed with the captain, though, the native was disconcertingly barbaric. Many tales circulated about Umgah, the Deke's personal tracker, and why it was that the Dyak would work for no other team commander. Rumours, spiced with truth, claimed that the Dyak was paid for his services in human heads.

Umgah the Dyak was a primitive at heart but far too sensible to rely on 'heads' to secure his future. Besides, his 'collection' had been lost too many times, as a squirrel will lose its store of autumn nuts. Though he retained an ingrained penchant for decapitating dead enemies, he had abandoned his practice of lugging the heads away, and left them on the battlefields as grisly trademarks. He took his 'wedges' now like other tribal natives in food, tobacco and Straits dollars.

Umgah showed Deacon his teeth. It was hardly a smile and certainly not a grimace but akin to the facial expression of certain types of ape.

Deacon went down on his belly by the Dyak's side.

'Hear sounds, Umgah?'

'Yeh.'

'Could it be an ox-cart column?'

'Yeh.'

'How far away?'

Umgah held up two fingers and crossed them with his thumb.

P.B., crouched by Deacon's side, interpreted. 'Closer'n two miles.'

'How many carts?' Deacon asked optimistically.

The Dyak expanded his yellow eyeballs and pursed his lips.

'Many?' Deacon revised the question.

'Menny,' the Dyak agreed.

Umgah and Johnny Badhur had been on watch since dawn. Each morning two of the team, Deacon included, took an early shift by the track. It was an imperfect system, wearing in the extreme, but Deacon could think of no other which would suit the circumstances. Damn it, it seemed to have worked well enough.

Luck was on their side after all.

Deacon rolled away from Umgah and positioned himself by the Gurkha.

'How are you feeling, Johnny?'

'In excellent health, sir.'

'Well enough to make a sprint back to the radio unit?'

'It will be no problem for me,' said the Gurkha Sergeant modestly.

'As arranged,' said Deacon, 'you and P.B. find a spy-hole on the other side of the track. Count the number of carts and the number of gun-carrying guards then slip away quietly.'

'At what time shall I request the RAF bomb drop?'

Deacon hesitated. He had no idea how far from Shan's base they were or how long it would take for the carts to reach it. In such deep country the bomb runs would have to be targeted exactly to be effective. There were four smoke flares in his Bergen and Buz had a couple of phosphor bombs to set grass or trees alight. It was probable that Shan would have spread the camp over a wide area but storage huts and armoury must somehow be accurately marked for the pilots. While the Gurkha and the Scot sped back to the radio, the Dyak, Buz and he would trail the carts at a discreet distance. In the wake of the bomb run they would lie low until a support party arrived, then they would endeavour to take prisoners. Prisoners were important sources of high-grade information.

Deacon checked his wrist-watch. It was twenty-five minutes past eight o'clock. He made a rough calculation. Bukit Basar was eight miles away and the ox-cart train would travel at a maximum of two miles in the hour.

'Two o'clock, Johnny. Fourteen hundred hours. No earlier, but not much later. Pass a message to the RAF to brief the pilots to take bearing on Bukit Basar and eyeball it from there.'

'What if it is raining and there is low cloud?'

'Another damned Jonah,' said Deacon.

'I do not understand, Jeff,' said the Gurkha.

'*You* won't be flying the planes, Johnny,' said Deacon. 'Deliver the message to the radio op. and leave the rest to the RAF.'

Solemnly the Gurkha nodded.

P.B. said, 'Better if we get out now, Johnny.'

Deacon said, 'Be careful. Take no chances. You've got to reach "Nelson".'

For some reason the Beezer had named the four teams after famous seamen; a man who was capable of dreaming up 'Bogwater' was capable of anything. The groups were 'Nelson', 'Drake', 'Raleigh' and, for Deacon's team, 'Jellicoe'. At least it gave the chaps something else to grumble about during the interminable waiting periods.

P.B. and Johnny Badhur slid away through the grass like

lizards. Seconds later there was no sign at all of the soldiers. Deacon could only surmise that they had found position across the track. It was unlikely that the ox-cart column would be heavily guarded, even more unlikely that the guards would be combing the brush. If they had made many monthly deliveries without interference they would probably be rather complacent.

Buz Campbell and the Dyak had found good cover. Deacon settled, not belly length but on all fours. At times like this, when any movement might telegraph their presence to the enemy, the insects became deadly. Flapping the fingers silently at them was ineffectual. But a slap might be heard on the track, even through the creak of cart-wheels and the grunting of draught animals.

Riding on a sea of ferns and *lalang* the carts appeared in single file.

Nobody had as yet defined what animals were yoked to the shafts. From cautious glimpses Deacon saw that they were indeed oxen, a domestic type of the semi-wild *bantings*, distinguishable by their whitish legs and rumps and comparatively small stature. Dainty beasts, they seemed to draw the high, box-sided, two-wheeled carts effortlessly.

The carts were laden, cargoes roped under tight, green-canvas tarps. They were identical with the produce vehicles that one could see in all parts of Malaya but minus the usual bamboo or palm-leaf awnings. The oxen were not paired abreast, however. They were roped snout to tail on cross yokes from an extended central drag pole, something Deacon had never seen before. It appeared to make little difference to the rate of progress. The carts were moving steadily enough. Two Malayan Chinese, hardly more than boys, walked ahead of the column carrying Japanese submachine-guns at the port. They were dressed in duck pants and open cotton shirts but sported the blunt American Army-style helmets which many CTs now favoured.

The carts were also driven by young men, one to each board. They wore floppy cotton jungle hats or broad-brimmed straws. They weren't armed, as far as Deacon could make out.

Nose lifted to a level with the clumps of grass and soft palmlings which sprouted on the rim of the depression, Deacon counted. Six, seven, eight carts; not so many as he had been led to believe. He wondered what lay under the canvases. Fresh food and canned goods? It would not surprise him to find American GI 'rations' there. The black market out of Korea was strong and inventive, its racketeers quite unscrupulous. No more than a dozen armed guerrillas accompanied the column. They wouldn't be tough monkeys. Some would be bound to crack under Special Branch interrogation. At least they would find out where the shipment came from, whatever else.

The ox-carts trundled past and disappeared.

Deacon sat back on his heels, laid down his gun and removed his beret. He swabbed his face with it. He felt as if every blasted mosquito in Malaya had a bite at him. He spat on his fingertips and rubbed his eyelids with saliva. He could afford to indulge himself in a concern for comfort for a while. There was no more to be done for a quarter of an hour or more. They must let the supply train wend on.

He glanced up at the sky through the trees. No sign of rain. Even if it poured, however, the Dyak would be able to follow the trail. Indeed, any of the three of them could follow the trail with its smashed fern stalks, hoof prints and dung, plus the indentations of eight pairs of broad wheels.

Buz appeared out of the grass. 'P.B. and Johnny get off okay?'

'I expect so,' Deacon whispered.

The sergeant jerked his thumb. 'Looks good, Deke.'

'Absolutely marvellous.'

'Trail 'em up at a safe distance and we can't miss.'

'Do you want a drink?'

'Sure. What is it?'

'Gin, I'm afraid.'

'Gin'll do.'

Fifteen minutes later, rested and refreshed, the three men padded down on to the track and, with the Dyak in the van, started cautiously after the CT supply column.

Man or woman, young or old, it made no difference to Umgah. With his wide nostrils flared, he could smell CTs miles off.

In a garbled conversation with P.B. McNair he had explained that each person has an odour which comes from the spirit – by which the Dyak did not mean good Scotch whisky. God knows what sort of spiritual aroma the girl gave off. She was dead before Buz and the Deke got to the spot, though the Dyak had been no more than twenty paces ahead of them. He had slit her slender throat with the blade of the parang, gripping the back of the blade as if it was a gigantic razor.

The girl never knew what hit her.

There was enough of the gentleman in Jeffrey Alexander Deacon to occasion a pang of regret and a degree of guilt at the killing of a girl.

The girl had been on guard. She had put down her rifle. It was a semi-automatic which at first glance looked like an American Garand but turned out to be one of the modified copies which the Japanese naval arsenal at Kure had cranked out in the last year of the Pacific war. She had been making water when Umgah nabbed her. Though she seemed very young, Deacon had no doubt at all that she would have shot them if she had spotted them first. She would not be an innocent virgin but a wife or girl-friend of one of the bandits. Perhaps she was even a section leader. There were several girls in the gangs and many more in the Min Yuen's District Unit branches. She seemed so small, though. The lack of dignity in her position disgruntled Deacon. He nodded at the Dyak in reluctant approval.

Stooping, Buz held the corpse with his elbow and rifled the girl's pockets. Pathetic little trophies came to light; lipstick and eyebrow pencil wrapped in a lace-edged handkerchief, two cheap rings in a chamois pouch. No letters, no photographs.

Deacon said, 'She's wearing a brassière, Sergeant.'

'Yeah. Yeah.'

With obvious distaste Buz bared the girl's chest and ran his finger round the cups of the garment.

'No dice,' Buz said. 'But this one's only the first, Deke.'

'Umgah.' The captain made a gesture of instruction.

The Dyak wiped the cleaver-like knife on the grass. He put the blade back into its open, leather envelope and caught the girl by the ankles and dragged her away from the track-side into the brush. He returned almost immediately.

The supply train had never been in sight. It was screened now by a stand of *jiring* trees whose limp young leaves hung in a crimson purple mass. The sun was hot and bright, however, and a sifting haze of dust marked the route. The shoulder of the Bukit Basar was visible above the palms, though there were no other signs to indicate that the guerrilla camp was close at hand. It was puzzling to find a scout so far out.

Deacon said, 'I hope to God she didn't have a friend with her.'

'Gel ner kampoung, *tuan*.'

'Are we, Umgah? Are we close?'

'Lench.'

'Lunch?' said Buz. 'What the hell . . .?'

'Sneff-sneff.' The Dyak touched his nose with the point of his spear.

'Do you smell cooking?' Deacon asked.

'Heh-yeh, *tuan* Deck.'

'Take the hint, Deke,' whispered Buz.

'All right,' said Deacon. 'But we'll stick together.'

'How come?'

'Because I'm suddenly rather nervous, old man.'

Buz grinned crookedly. 'Sure.'

'If we are on top of the encampment then we're obliged to sit tight until the planes arrive. It is, after all, only five minutes past eleven.'

'*Tiss-tiss*,' hissed the Dyak. He rolled his eyes towards the great gaudy spray of the *jiring* trees.

The bandit came around them without caution, full of lightness and love, ruttish as a bull. He carried a bamboo basket over his arm. It contained ripe fruits, cigarettes and a bottle of French wine, complete with label.

Captain and sergeant dropped to their bellies as the bandit cooed the girl's name. Perhaps he was city-born, not used to the dangers of the jungle. Perhaps he considered himself secure in this tropical Eden. It didn't take a genius to guess that he had just come off the end of the ox-cart train and that the girl had been awaiting her lover.

'Yin Tao? Yin Tao?' he called alluringly.

He glanced back over his shoulder to make sure that he had not been followed, that his assignation would be private. The dead girl – Yin Tao – might even have been somebody else's woman.

Deacon and Campbell pressed themselves into the scant grass. The bandit was too far away to knife. They did not dare risk a shot. Rifle fire would put up the hive. It was clear now that the camp was close to their hiding place. A startled cry, a shout of warning, a death scream, any sound would do it. This love-struck Chink could blow the entire operation.

'Damnation,' Deacon mouthed soundlessly.

'Yin Tao?' the bandit coaxed. 'Yiiin Taaao?'

Neither of the SAS men saw the occurrence. It was a repetition of the killing of the girl. As Buz put it, the goddamned Dyak sure earned his 'salt dollar' that morning.

The crimson purple leaves of the cluster of *jiring* shivered.

'Yin T—'

The shrill voice cut off without so much as a squeak.

The Dyak did not use his knife. He slotted the shorter of his two war spears into the bandit's back, driving it through the spinal column. One large hand was clamped over the bandit's gaping mouth. With a jerk, Umgah extracted the spear. He let the bandit's body sink to the ground. With his foot he rolled the corpse under the leaves of the *jiring* trees.

Deacon peered over the tops of the grasses.

'Dear God!'

Umgah raised his spear and did a brisk little dance of triumph.

Deacon and Campbell got to their feet.

Deacon praised the Dyak, patting his shoulder as a father might express approval to a child. The Dyak enjoyed being popular. But there was no time to waste; God knows how many other bandits were 'straying' about the bush.

Taking a diagonal left of the track, the Dyak led off again. The swamp was below them but the hot febrile stench of the Totan rode the lighter air of the hill country. It was a queer, mixed area, this north corner of the Totan, without fields or ore pits or any sort of commercial nexus. Neglected was the word for it.

Conscious of the fact that Shan might have set traps around the perimeter of the camp the three men moved carefully. More than one British soldier had died by crashing into a pit or stepping on a mine. Shan's experts in deadly devices, ancient and modern, were very good at their job.

After a trek of three or four hundred yards, the ground rose to a hummocky crest overgrown with starweed and a species of thin-leaved ivy. Deacon sent Buz on ahead. The sergeant bellied over the hummock, putting up a flock of minute white butterflies which fluttered like snowflakes in the humid air. Crouching, Deacon and the Dyak watched Buz disappear. Seconds later, the sergeant's arm showed over the vivid green leaves and he signalled his companions forward.

Beyond the leafed hummock was the tail of Sand Shan's encampment. A beaten track under dwarf palms straggled into mangosteens and big old dadaps which, at this season, had forced out their curious seed pods. The track lay in a tunnel of trees and would be totally invisible from the air. Along the inner side of the hummock were two shallow bunkers and a Bren-gun bench fashioned from logs. The defences were empty, however. It was by no means unusual for CT encampments to be ringed by defensive earthworks. In this past year or so, with greatly increased activity on the part of the Security Forces, several guerrilla leaders had been forced to make a stand. Open warfare suited the experienced British soldiers very well. Sand Shan, though, had not bothered to man his rearward positions at the noon hour. On the far side of the beaten area was a canvas awning. The acrid stink indicated that it was or had been a latrine. Beyond it, left, was a rubbish pit. One could learn a lot from inspection of a garrison's debris but Deacon had neither the time nor the inclination to rummage that morning. Besides, the pit was clouded with flies and stalked by birds of one sort or another, including a couple of vultures.

Hand cupped over his mouth, Buz murmured, 'What do you reckon?'

Deacon nodded at the ramp of trees behind the latrine. 'Backside of the Bukit Basar, I think.'

'Yeah.'

The hill surveyed at 420 feet, which was hardly high. But it gave some kind of shape to the undulations of the prickly swamp country. Besides, Bukit Basar was more of a low range than a single hill. It stretched several miles east. No rock was visible along its shoulders, which were matted with vegetation. The guerrilla camp must cover several acres. The dumps in which the SAS were particularly interested would be at the heart of it, skilfully camouflaged.

'Up,' said Deacon, 'for a looksee?'

Buz nodded.

The Dyak fell to the rear as the three men crabbed across the beaten earth and into the ferns behind the old latrine.

They moved up into the dadaps which, with the flowering season just past, were coated with dried flowers like crusts of blood. The men climbed a couple of hundred feet then traversed to the south-east around the breast of the hill.

Voices were audible below and to the right. Sago palms and padans usurped the dadaps. There was a stand of unhealthy-looking bamboo which the SAS men skirted on the high side. No bunkers, fox-holes or watch stations were to be seen. The upper slopes of the Bukit Basar did not appear to be utilised by the guerrillas.

Deciduous trees in the uniform climate of Malaya had no regular seasonal calendar and shed leaves willy-nilly. Sunlight penetrated a lattice of naked boughs where wild rubber had shed in the drought which preceded the sumatra rains. Sunlight angled steeply as if through a series of Norman windows, and the naves of gold and emerald light were breathtaking. Deacon was in no mood to appreciate beauty. Quickly he found a vantage point from which he could peer down on the encampment and gain some idea of its topography.

Running east was a narrow-necked jungle valley down which, the maps indicated, the river gathered itself. The whole sprawl of the camp, though, was sheltered by stands of tall trees. Undergrowth had been cleaned and thatch shelters built, quite solid structures. An earth bank and a sand-strewn square were crowded with CTs in process of unloading the carts which were drawn up on its edge.

Buz whispered, 'What've they got, Deke?'

Deacon extracted a powerful monocular from its case and held it to his eye. He took focus. He scanned the ants' nest of activity carefully.

'Guns. Packed in crates. Something . . . Dear God, explosives.'

'You're kiddin'?'

'Absolutely not. Quite a parcel of it. See for yourself.'

Deacon passed the monocular to Buz who adjusted the lens and studied the scene.

'Jesus! US Army crates. You make out the stencils? Straight from Uncle Sam's warehouses.'

'Yes,' whispered Deacon.

'Canned goodies, too. Beer, Coke. Shit, that looks like cartons of Campbell's soups.'

'I wouldn't be surprised,' said Deacon. 'Clearly our friend Mr Shan has a first-class supply officer in one of the cities.'

Buz handed back the glass.

Dropping lower on the hillside, the three men crept from vantage point to vantage point while unloading continued.

Foodstuffs were stored in palm-thatch huts with open sides, shelved to keep the rats away. But weapons and explosives were being toted close to the hillside. It was a quarter of an hour before Deacon succeeded in spying out the dumps, log-shored bunkers set deep into the earth. Shaded by awnings fashioned from camouflage netting and tarpaulins, the arsenal was at the eastern end of the encampment.

Training had been interrupted by the arrival of the supply train. But the sites were visible. Bayonet dummies were staked on a sanded pad. A shooting range with hanging targets funnelled across a wing of the jungle. Billeting was mostly in pup and ridge tents and a buffet-like kitchen with four serving trestles and a range of big, smokeless kerosene cookers stood close to the main concentration. In all, Deacon judged that there must be three hundred bandits permanently stationed here, girls as well as men. It would have been instructive to watch them training, to gauge the quality and learn just how efficient Shan's soldiers had become. But reconnaissance had eaten away time and, with the RAF bombers due in sixty-five minutes, Deacon must act.

Through the glass the captain had spotted two obvious break-out points, across the jungle clearing by the range, and down the corkscrew track into the head of the valley. There was also the ox-cart track, but somehow Deacon supposed that Shan would not use it in the event of a raid. Gallingly, Deacon had not sighted Sand Shan, though his second-in-command, the towering Kwai Yan Chung, was strutting up and down, bossing the porters. Cart drivers were being fed. They squatted over their mess tins by the kitchen. The oxen had been unharnessed and led off to a grazing out of Deacon's sight.

'Figure Shan's here?' Buz Campbell asked.

'No. I think we're out of luck yet again.'

'What's the score, Deke?'

'Blow the explosives. Hope that the RAF can hit the goodies smack on. And make sure that we take the big fellow alive. He's our target, Buz. If it's humanly possible, then we must try to isolate and grab Kwai Yan Chung – assuming, that is, that we can't have Shan himself.'

'Shan'd have been out an' about by now, right?'

'Probably,' said Deacon.

'Christ, but he's slippery.'

'Sadly true.'

'Maybe the boys in the backroom can make Goliath squawk.'

'The important thing under the circumstances is to destroy the arsenal. That's bound to hurt. If only the damned place wasn't so far up country we could have mounted a full-scale attack against it. Marching fire, that sort of thing.'

'Hell, Deke,' said Buz, 'we should count our blessin's. This time yesterday we figured the op. was gonna fizzle out. I say grab what we can an' be glad of it.'

'Of course,' said the captain.

Buz said, 'Tell Umgah we want the big man alive. Not his bloody head; all of him.'

Deacon informed the Dyak of their intentions while Buz prepared a string of grenades and loaded a Vaughan shotgun and a Browning automatic pistol he had brought with him as part of his personal armoury. The shotgun was an exceptionally useful weapon at close quarters. Buz used one whenever he could, in spite of its carrying weight. The current model had been a gift from a planter's wife, the Wingfield woman.

To an outsider the plan might have seemed too simple, almost suicidal. Buz would slip down the hillside and enter the back of the tarps which covered the ammo dump. He would rig a grenade string and sit tight until five minutes to two o'clock by his watch. He would detonate the fast fuses, emerge from the dump and run like crazy back up the hill to the spot where Deacon was waiting to give him cover. If P.B. and the Gurkha *had* made it on time and if the radio message *had* gotten through to the RAF strip at Taiman, sixty miles to the south, then the dump would blow sky high just as the bombers appeared in the area. Blowing the dump would serve as a marker. As soon as the bombing run was completed, Buz, Deacon and Umgah would try to pick up Kwai Yan Chung and nail him.

Back-up units, 'K' and 'A' Squadron gunners, would be travelling fast towards the location, following the wet track through the Totan that P.B. and Johnny had established.

Deacon was confident that the groups would net any CTs who headed down the cart trail.

'You know what to do, Buz?'

'Sure.'

'You have fifty minutes.'

'Right.'

'Keep your head down, Sergeant.'

'Right.'

Deacon watched Buz creep down the hillside and vanish into the lush undergrowth at the back of the dumps. There appeared to be no guards positioned around the dumps which was uncommonly careless of Sand Shan. If the cat was away, however, perhaps the mice tended to be less than cautious. On the other hand, there might be a Chink or two within the dumps, in which case Buz would be in trouble.

Tensely, Deacon held the spy-glass steady, trained on the camouflaged roofs of the bunkers. He could not see them well. Activity around them had ceased. Most of the CTs seemed to be feeding, sprawled about the camp area to his right. He sent the Dyak through the bush to keep an eye on the main area. Umgah returned in ten minutes. He made eating signals. Perhaps there had also been a mail delivery. The guerrillas would be absorbed in reading letters from their mothers, girl-friends and wives.

It was now twenty-two minutes to two o'clock.

Waiting stretched Deacon's nerves like frayed elastic. He felt as if he might snap at any moment. He had been a mite too long in the swamp country. He had the feeling that if Sand Shan appeared below him right now, he might throw caution, training and common-sense to the winds and shoot the little bastard through the head. It would not be a difficult shot for a marksman. At this range, even with a downhill slope to contend with, P.B. could shoot the eyes out of a bullfrog. No wind and a hot, heavy atmosphere.

Sweat dripped from Deacon's brows and trickled down his nose, an aristocratic patrician beak common to all his family and visible in portraits of the Baronets of Rathbone going back three centuries.

On the far side of the clearing, by the unseen butts of the shooting range, two female guerrillas unwrapped a cardboard box and held up a sarong. Mail order for terrorists? What next! Without scruple, Jeffrey Alexander Deacon spied on the girls through the glass. He watched one unbutton her duck trousers and step out of them. She had plump legs and a round belly. She fitted on the sarong, a gaudy garment in bright reds and yellows, and preened in front of her companion.

Rest and relaxation: siesta time in the butcher's back closet.

It would be a different story in a quarter of an hour.

Many of the guerrillas would die, many more would be wounded. The plump girl might never have the chance to show off her new sarong. Deacon felt no pity and no remorse. He was almost immune to it now. He had seen too many horrors in his years in Malaya. Male or female, old or young, Communist Terrorists were as dangerous as cobras and deserved to be stamped out.

By Deacon's side the Dyak shifted his weight on to his right knee and elevated his short spear from the ground. Deacon followed the pointing spear. Something was coming towards them. He held the Sten against his hip, finger on the trigger, then let out his breath in relief as Buz Campbell's sweaty face appeared through the fern stalks.

'I thought—' Deacon whispered.

Buz rolled on to his back. His shirt was black with sweat and his cheeks glowed dusky red. He motioned to Deacon to come close. The captain leaned over him on all fours. Buz grinned.

'All done. No problem. Joint's stacked with high explosives. Dynamite, plastic, you name it. Boxed and aired. Fuses too. Hundreds of them. And timers.'

'Did you set a time fuse?'

'Goddamned right. Tick-tick.'

'Will it work? Is it reliable?'

'Best quality. American.'

'Good God!'

'Two o'clock on the nose, Deke. We'd better get the hell out of here. This is far too close for comfort, man.'

Buz rolled on to his knees, like a bear. Grinning, the Dyak waited. He had understood the gist of the sergeant's account.

'Wait.' Deacon swivelled and made a last sweeping survey of the encampment.

The guerrillas were beginning to stir themselves. A dozen or more were wending towards a dip, the stream perhaps. There was some laughter. It might have been anybody's army on manoeuvres, apart from the girls and the fact that the men were as small as children. He saw Kwai Yan Chung, smoking a cigar, talking to two of the ox-cart drivers. The huge Chinese had put on a cowboy hat, a Stetson. He carried an ugly, heavy-weight machine-gun in his left hand as easily as if it was a pistol.

Nine minutes short of two o'clock.

'Over the side of the hill, Deke, I'm tellin' yuh.'

Deacon let the sergeant lead, trekking up through dense timber, north-east towards the summit of the Bukit and, with increasing urgency, across it. No smoke canisters had been set, no alternative measures taken. Deacon put his trust in Buz Campbell and Buz put his trust in the fuses. If somebody happened to go into the explosives bunker, find the timer fuse – the bomber pilots would have no markers at all. They would drone over the camp without releasing.

'Hey, look at that, now,' Buz said, panting.

They had come across the crown of the hill and had sight of the narrow-throated valley. The river lay like a twist of silver foil in the sunlight, the Sungai Konyang. It linked the swamp with the far-distant plain. It was swollen with the recent rains, fed by three or four dashing tributaries which would not normally be visible.

'You see what I see?' said Buz.

'What?'

Umgah nudged the Deke's shoulder and pointed.

The camouflage of thatch and leaves was intended to hide the canoes from the air. From this vantage point, only three hundred yards or so above the bamboo jetty, the craft were fairly easy to spot. Moored to tree roots, the canoes were big jobs, high-riders. Deacon had seen similar ones in shallow-water fishing villages up on the delta by Selinsing Bay. Only these were not painted in bold primary colours but had been camouflaged with green and mud-brown paint. Eight boats waved and weaved restlessly with the drizzle of the current in the shallows by the jetty.

And no guards. No damned guards.

Deacon could hardly believe it. Shan had really cocked up. Had the guerrilla leader been so confident that the Seeurity Forces wouldn't find the Totan encampment that he had neglected even elementary precautions? It seemed so – unless, of course, Shan was far away and Kwai Yan Chung was the casual sort.

Deacon said, 'It's like that bloody 'copter again.'

Deacon had almost had Sand Shan in his clutches once before, after a successful 'back door' counter-attack on the Wade-Wingfield plantation but, out of nowhere, Wei Sand Shan had produced a helicopter to whisk him away from the battlefield.

'Sure does it right, don't he?' said Buz.

'Who gets the places in the boats?'

Buz shrugged. 'The boss-men, officers, the ones who can't be replaced. Weapons experts and radio wallahs and guys who can handle explosives. Take maybe forty out, I figure.'

'Including,' said Deacon, 'Kwai Yan Chung.'

The first of three RAF Hawker Tempests hurtled over the ridge.

'Christ!' Buz exclaimed. 'What the hell time is it?'

'Fourteen hundred hours,' said Deacon. 'Exactly.'

'Then hit the deck,' cried Buz.

In the opinion of many experienced combat pilots, the Hawker Tempest Mk. V was the finest ground-attack aircraft ever built. The single-seater fighter bomber had four 20 mm cannons and could discharge 2,000 lbs worth of bombs through a hatch perfectly positioned below the pilot's feet. You could feel the *thunk* of the missiles and get a sure sense of target position just the way you could with darts. Some flyers thought the plane was a shade long in the tooth, but the handful of the type in service in Malaya proved otherwise. The plane was ideal for anti-guerrilla attacks on pin-point positions in deep jungle. *Blast 'em out and gun 'em down* was the pilots' motto, and Hawker Tempests were superb machines for the job. The three planes came in a staggered V formation, skimming the trees, banking along the shoulders of the Bukit Basar, banking high and coming round once more over the camp. Since the weather was fine, the pilots would be flying by their eyeballs not by instruments, peering in search of the promised marker.

All three planes passed over the camp site again and vanished. The jungle absorbed the vibrations of the big Napier Sabre 24-cylinder engines like blotting paper. In the guerrilla encampment the scatter began. Deacon and Buz saw none of it. With the Dyak they were sprawled among the vegetation, arms wrapped over their heads.

Twenty seconds elapsed between the appearance of the planes and the first explosions. Shock riddled through the hillside. In front of the Deke's nose, stalks of fern shivered. A curtain of webs spun by an industrious spider ripped softly apart with the shudder of high-explosive detonations.

'Gotcha!' Buz shouted. 'On the friggin' nose, gotcha!'

'Operation Bogwater' had now justified all the planning and man-hours expended on it. Taking out one big CT arms dump was reward enough. But the exercise wasn't over yet, not by a long chalk.

'Bury it, Buz,' Deacon yelled as the sound of the planes grew, high-pitched, like a slash of silver against the dark brown rumble from the bunkers across the shoulder of the hill. *'Heads down.'*

The Dyak had his eyes squeezed shut. He held on to a spear with each hand, as if to rails.

The RAF pilots knew their business.

One of the Tempests strewed the base of the Bukit with bombs while the chasing planes pumped out cannon shells.

They not only had the great column of earth and smoke still hanging in the air above the jungle to give them target centre, they could see the enemy below – figures breaking through the cover, out of and through the camouflage. The strike pattern could not have been better.

Down into the snuggle of the valley head and up again in a series of three beautiful looped turns which brought them back out of the sun in reverse pattern, the planes seeded another package of bombs and another prong of cannon shells.

Fire – the kitchen stoves – flashed. Four small, intense explosions rocked the earth. The CTs, few of whom had ever experienced an air raid, turned out to be anything but stoical. They fled in panic. From the jungle, like a warped sound-track, emerged all kinds of bird and animal noises. A flock of hill mynahs winged away like smoke-smuts. Five barking deer thundered lightly out of the trees, swerving and leaping, near the spot where the SAS men crouched. The planes made a final strafing run – and then were gone, the roar of their engines, feathered by the trees, fading fast.

Deacon was on his knees, lens trained. From this position he could not see the camp area well, only the tail of it. But there was heavy smoke of various hues floating over the trees and the snarl of fire was audible. The CTs were in full flight. If they had been drilled in defence measures they had forgotten their training.

'Oh, boy! Oh, brother!' Buz Campbell adjusted a Sten on its barrel tripod. 'Fish in a friggin' barrel.'

'Wait,' said Deacon.

'Jesus, Deke—'

'Wait.'

There would be time for spot shooting later. Deacon had not abandoned hope that the bombing would flush out Sand Shan, that the Red Number One had been hidden in one of the tents and would be making for the canoes. Again the captain cursed the fact that there was no heavily-armed platoon in the region. The haul in lives, in prisoners, would have been terrific. Headline news for the *Straits Times.*

If there was no Shan, however, Kwai Yan Chung would have to do instead.

At times like these, there was a decided disadvantage in being a foot taller than any of your countrymen. Kwai Yan Chung was all too obvious. He came on the heels of a phalanx of armed and uniformed guards which doubled towards the jetty, exactly a dozen of them.

Poor rank-and-file bastards who sprinted to the river were fired upon, sprayed at random with automatic weapons. They fell away, dropping into the water or crawling into the brush. Boats were for big fellows, boss-men. The spirit of Communism was nowhere in evidence. The pecking order was ruthlessly enforced. Wounded had no priority. Kwai Yan Chung and his twelve special guards would be out of the area within minutes.

'Yeah, yeah! I got it, Deke,' said Buz Campbell. 'But why the hell're they running so hard? I mean, they gotta have it figured the raid's over.'

'They over-estimate us,' said Deacon. 'They think we have land forces ready to swarm all over them. Obviously the Tempests did a great deal of damage.'

'Right.'

Kwai Yan Chung's entourage had almost reached the hidden jetty. Nets and thatch were flung aside, canoes floated free on their short moorings. Behind Kwai Yan Chung came a reasonably well-organised group. Four signal corps officers carried a big, boxy radio on a litter, a high-powered job with a crank-handle generator. Next came three women with satchels – codebooks and paymaster's ledgers? – then a line of officers and NCOs, confident, even cocky. Three were wounded. One was being carried by another. Deacon concentrated on Kwai Yan Chung.

'Grenades, Buz.'

'Yep.'

'Make sure you get the radio.'

'Yep.'

'Umgah?'

'Tuan.'

'You, me – river. Okay?'

'Okey, keptin *tuan*.'

'Buz, take them out as clean as you can.'

'Right, Deke. You goin' for the big guy?'

'Of course.'

'I'll give you cover from the left bank.'

'If we capture him from the canoe,' said Deacon, 'I'll haul him into the jungle and hold him there until the hoo-ha dies down. You lie low too, Buz, then make a wide detour and try to contact our back-up units. They should be on the way by now.'

'Got you.' Buz grinned. 'Some birthday, uh?'

'Better than pipe and slippers, Buz.'

'Maybe.' Buz Campbell gripped the captain's arm and added with great seriousness, 'Listen – anything happens – you know – look after the kid. Look after Susu.'

'You have my promise.'

'See you around.'

During the conversation the SAS men had not been idle. They knew precisely what to do and what risks were involved.

They had the advantage of surprise and superior position. The camp was badly damaged and the bandits in a state of confusion. Even so, they were massively outnumbered. Sudden, daring strikes and swift retreat into the jungle would be essential. Buz would be the key factor, the sergeant's ability to make every grenade count, every shot find a target, convincing the group by the boats that he was a whole goddamned platoon.

Deacon and the Dyak slid through the trees down to the straggling bank of the Sungai Konyang.

Kwai Yan Chung was in the lead canoe. Another piece of luck. None of this crap about an officer making way for his men. Couldn't blame the Chink. The quality of recruits in training was poor, if the response to the raid was anything to go by.

Buz lowered himself on to his belly. Dragging a bag of grenades as well as the shotgun and Sten, he did his worm act through the ferns. Instinct told him when he was close enough. There were a dozen good guns on the other side of the river, which was no more than twenty yards wide, shallow and muddy, with a splash pool on his right. Buz held the grass blades apart and peered between them.

Kwai Yan Chung was seated in the canoe. Amidships. He ignored the chattering Chinks. He directed the loading of the radio into a second canoe. Four signal corps guys got in with it. Two uniformed guards put down their guns and swung out the long bamboo poles. It didn't seem to matter to the guerrilla commander what was happening to the other canoes. They were filling up with polers and guards and officers. The three women with the big canvas satchels slung round them like mailmen had an honoured place. Kwai Yan Chung looked back towards the camp just one time then he made a signal like a wagon-master in a Western movie.

Somebody unhitched the painter. The first canoe, containing Kwai Yan Chung and two guards, swung out into the sluggish current. The guards dipped their poles and dug for bottom. The nose of the craft came around. Behind there was a hellish scramble. Gun shots. Shrieks. One screaming native with a hole in his side.

Kwai Yan Chung floated clear of the bank.

From now on the capture of Red Number Two was Deacon's business.

Mouth dry, teeth clenched, big Buz Campbell jerked the pins from two hand-grenades. He lay back against the slope of the hill and lobbed each of the grenades overhand without showing himself.

He closed his eyes for an instant. Saw a fleeting vision of Susu, sweet and smiling, her slanted eyes full of mischief and desire.

The grenades exploded in water.

There was screaming.

Buz opened his eyes. He rolled on to his hip and fired a burst from the Sten, a long, sustained burst through the thin grasses into the bunch of guerrillas that swarmed about the boats. He rolled again and, dragging the guns and the grenade bag, headed for another hide downstream aways – to do it all again.

*

Deacon and the Dyak had covered a couple of hundred yards before Buz commenced his attack. The jungle was thick, thorn bushes knotted with creeper, trees festooned with fleshy moss. It was difficult to tell where the fall-off to the river lay and Deacon drew the Dyak back and down. Firing. Several volleys. Staccato chatter of a Sten or a Browning. Another couple of grenades, the laboured creak of a tree and a leafy crash as it fell. The canoes had been hit, that much Deacon could make out. Only three boats had cleared the bank. They were drifting on down towards him.

The big Chinese, Kwai Yan Chung, was looking back, one arm upraised to shield his forehead. He wore a lid now but the ridiculous Stetson was on his back on its strap. He had produced a hand-gun, a long-barrelled magnum which he held in his right hand at shoulder level. The guards were scared. They poled carelessly, without rhythm. In the second canoe the radio had become a barricade for the signallers crouched around it. They had rifles, though. The three girls in the third canoe were also armed.

Umgah took in the situation at a glance. He seemed awfully calm. His broad chest rose and fell and he had a gleam in his eye which Deacon recognised.

'What?' Deacon whispered.

'Heh-heh,' said the Dyak softly. 'Umgah watter. Yew gens.'

'Gens?'

'Banga-banga.'

Deacon nodded his understanding.

From up-river came further bursts of shooting and another explosion. Buz had found a new, safe position and was making mincemeat of the bandits on the far bank. Like a crocodile Umgah waddled belly down through the vegetation and into the mud of the river. He was some forty yards below the lead craft. The guards had discarded their bamboo poles in favour of paddles and were endeavouring to find the rhythm they had lost. They had no opportunity to do so.

Deacon watched the swirl of the water for a moment, glimpsed the Dyak's broad back, and began his attack.

The Sungai Konyang wasn't rapid enough to carry the canoes swiftly out of range. Deacon strafed the second and third boats, then, standing, pitched a grenade at each of them. He was breast-deep in jungle growth and had no run-up. Even so he found target with one grenade and saw the signallers scramble to get out of the canoe. Still standing, Deacon squeezed the trigger of his Sten-gun. The CTs flopped and fell into each other. The canoe dithered off line, nosing a degree or two towards the bank before it was blown apart. Wood splintered. A split-second later the craft wallowed, pitching the bandits and the big radio into the river.

At the same instant a spout of brown water showered the third craft. The three female insurgents were spunky, however, and returned fire. Bullets plucked into the leaves around Deacon's head. But the girls were blinded by river water and the captain seized the opportunity to improve his position. He dived forward and into the ooze and, standing on the gnarled roots of a palm tree, blazed into the squall of brown water and smoke trace.

When the canoe floated out and became visible there was nobody left alive in it.

The Dyak had gone armed with traditional weapons, a spear and a knife. Deacon did not see the action. How the two paddlers were disposed of was a minor mystery. With the spear, probably. By the time the captain turned his attention to the lead canoe, Umgah was in complete command.

Umgah held the spear tucked into his armpit like a lance. The short, leaf-shaped blade pointed directly at Kwai Yan Chung's breastbone. The CT had his hands in the air. There was no sign at all of the guards. It was as if the Dyak had swallowed them whole. Paddling with one arm, the Dyak steered the canoe towards the shore.

Deacon scanned the surface of the river. Bodies floated. One girl had fallen overboard and thrashed at the water, blood flowering on her shirt, frail arms ineffectually beating. Deacon did not fire again. It was not in his nature to kill unarmed wounded. He watched the girl for a moment longer, saw her swing with the current and clutch at an overhanging branch. She crooked an elbow round it. The blood patch on her shirt was very red.

'Keptin tuan.'

Deacon switched his attention to Umgah and his prisoner, the hulking Chinese officer, Wei Sand Shan's right-hand man. The canoe came broadside against the rim of mud. Umgah grabbed a handful of weeds. Splashing down the edge of the river, Deacon spread his legs and trained the Sten on Kwai Yan Chung. The Chinese glared balefully at him.

Kwai Yan Chung was older than Deacon had imagined. He had studied photographs of the rebel officer and had read up on what was known of his history. A fanatical communist, he had studied in many theatres of war. Kwai Yan Chung had held official posts in the Pan-Malayan Communist Federation until his 'hate' policies had conflicted with the majority line. After his departure from the semi-formal structure of the political core, he had linked with Wei Sand Shan. It was rumoured that Yan Chung was responsible for the establishment and training of the special 'killer squads' which had wreaked so much havoc with the planters and miners in Selangor and Perak. For the last ten months Kwai Yan Chung, like his master Sand Shan, had been 'invisible' to the eyes and ears of the Security Forces.

Deacon said, 'Do you speak English?'

Kwai Yan Chung did not answer. An answer was unnecessary. Deacon remembered from the dossier on the man that his English was excellent.

Deacon said, 'Climb out of the boat very slowly, Yan Chung. I will not hesitate to shoot you, and my Dyak is very impetuous.'

Kwai Yan Chung's bulk, Deacon observed, was mostly muscle. He had the build of a professional wrestler with a big belly and short, powerful thighs. His expression was one of derisive defiance, but he obeyed the order smartly enough.

Deacon stepped into the water and kicked the stern of the canoe with his knee, sent it out into the current. At spear-point Umgah prodded the Red into the cover of the undergrowth out of sight of the river. Deacon followed.

There were no trails here. The ground climbed steeply through high, dragging growths up to the summit of the Bukit Basar. The SAS officer had no need to tell the Dyak what they were looking for – a safe hiding place, a shelter where they could lie up until the first troops from 'K' squadron arrived and Yan Chung could be handed over and ferried safely out of the wilderness. The man was a prize catch. Intelligence and Police officers would all have a 'pick' at him. His interrogation would last for many weeks, months perhaps. Eventually he would be charged and brought to trial and, when found guilty, executed. Deacon would have little or no part in any of that. He did not for a moment doubt that Kwai Yan Chung would be found guilty of many crimes, including murder, even if witnesses were hard to find. The trapping and capture of Kwai Yan Chung and the destruction of the arsenal at the Totan were coups which would enhance Deacon's already considerable reputation. The manner of it would add to the legend. None of this mattered to Jeffrey Alexander Deacon.

Deacon did not care a jot for personal glory. He found HQ politics and Colonial administration a bore. What he wanted out of it, his reward if you like, was a clue to the whereabouts of Wei Sand Shan, the boss, the butcher, the invisible warrior. He wanted Shan where Yan Chung was now, at the end of a gun.

There were rocks here, grey as elephant hide, and a dry basin with velvet grass on its rim and a cover of palm fronds. It was one of those strange, exotic spots which one stumbled across in the jungle, particularly where the ground was firm and rose towards the sky.

Deacon said, 'This will do. Umgah, tie his hands.'

The Dyak took two pieces of cord from around his waist and deftly lashed Kwai Yan Chung's hands together, knotting the cords at the wrists very tightly indeed. The Chinese neither helped nor hindered the process and, when told, sat down and extended his thick legs. The Dyak tied his ankles above the tops of the jungle boots. He did it expertly, with a hobble. Kwai Yan Chung did not watch the native's work. He did not appear to be watching Deacon either. But the SAS captain knew that his every move was being observed and evaluated. He kept himself a reasonable distance from the CT, the gun held tightly.

'If you shout,' said Deacon, 'I will have you gagged.'

Insolently the CT opened his mouth wide – but uttered no sound.

'And if you try to escape,' Deacon went on, 'I will shoot you.'

The CT pulled another face.

Gestures of arrogant defiance did not fool Deacon. Kwai Yan Chung knew he was in trouble, deep trouble – and he was afraid. Inside the barrel-shaped belly his guts were churning with nervousness, and inside the big chest his heart was pounding with fear.

Deacon said, 'Now we wait.'

Kwai Yan Chung said nothing.

It was nineteen hours before the first troops from 'K' Squadron stole into the encampment and, at the Canadian sergeant's insistence, loosed a volley of shots into the air.

An hour after that, a weary Deacon drove his prisoner off the Bukit Basar and turned him over to Captain Pawson who would ferry him, under heavy guard, all the way back to the Prince Albert Colonial Prison House in Port Kernan.

'Good God, Deacon, you look done in,' said Pawson.

'Been awake all night.'

'Have a bit of a kip,' said Pawson. 'I'll see to it that you're not disturbed.'

'Where are my men?'

'What men, old chap?'

'Sergeants Campbell and Badhur, and Corporal McNair.'

'Oh, they're here. Somewhere. I'm hanging on until 'A' Squadron arrives. I'll secure the camp and attend wounded prisoners but I'm not inclined to sally into the green stuff without a larger complement.'

'Of course.'

'I say, you do look rough. I'll find you a bed in a tent.'

'No,' Deacon said. 'Find my chaps and I'll start back at once.'

'The devil you will!'

'There's a whole day's light left. Sin to waste it.'

'Suit yourself, Deacon. What's the rush?'

'I just want to get home.'

'Missing the Beezer, are you?'

'Absolutely,' said Deacon.

Murder by demand

'Oh, so you're back at last,' said Major Cecil Beasley. 'Rewarding trip, I hear?'

'Yes, sir. Pawson's bringing back Yan Chung.'

'Damned good show.'

'I've been through debriefing, sir.'

'Good! Good! No sign of Shan in your wanderings?'

'No visible sign.'

'Disappointing, what?'

'Exceedingly,' said Deacon.

'Legged it back alone, did you?'

'With my team, Major.'

'Anxious to be out of it, what?'

'No, sir. But our work was done.'

'Who said your work was done?'

'I . . .'

'Who gave you authority, Captain?'

'I acted on my own authority, sir.'

'Quite right, too. Be off to the fleshpots now, I suppose.'

'If you feel I've earned a stand-down.'

'Of course you have. Good job. Well done.'

'Thank you, Major.'

'Three days all right?'

'Ideal.'

'Not off tiger shootin' or anything?'

'Bath and bed, Major.'

'Will you mess with us tonight, Captain?'

'If you wish it, sir.'

'You mean, if I order it, Deacon. No. No. You've earned your repose. Where will you be?'

'At the St John's.'

'I see.'

The Beezer gave a quick sniff of moral disapproval. He had never quite adjusted to the fact that his fighters lived lives of incredible contrast and regarded the Port Kernan garrison camp not as 'home' but as a stepping-off point into the jungle. Though a handful of officers were billeted in the mess – a handsome, white-painted building with a cool bar and an excellent kitchen – the majority of patrol leaders put up in one or other of the Port's hotels and were linked to general duties of the garrison only by military necessity.

The Beezer did not approve of the 'licentious behaviour' of his officers and non-coms but did not play the dictator too strenuously in this respect. He was conscious of the fact that the type of soldier under his command needed special treatment. Therefore he confined his mania for spit, polish and 'correctness' to base staff and let the fighting units have a long leash. He trusted his officers and instructors to see to it that they and their men did not go entirely to the bow-wows and remained fit to function at peak during the jungle hauls.

What went on behind the bamboo curtains of the Port's bars and hotels, the Beezer ignored. He put up no bans and posted few restrictions, and personally bore the onus of responsibility for security. There weren't many silly boys in his squadron. Lectures and discussions on the subject of 'leaks' and the constant need for caution in dealings with indigenous personnel were frequent, attendance compulsory.

The Beezer kept his own little black book. It wasn't filled with the names of 'available' ladies but with the juicier details of the private lives of his staff, non-coms included. On a small garrison, existing only to springboard deep penetration sorties like 'Operation Bogwater', and to assist the standard patrols of the Malayan Police, it wasn't difficult for the CO to acquire information on his chaps and the women his chaps consorted with. For instance he knew all about Sergeant Campbell's infatuation with the girl Susu Mafan, every detail of Compton-Sherret's ardent pursuit of Margaret McAnsh, wife of the manager of Owens' Land & Sea Freight Insurance Company, and, of course, of Deacon's association with the widow, Allison Wingfield, a relationship which was a marriage in all but name. Whatever longings and desires went through bachelor Beasley's mind remained veiled. He had no confidante in camp, or elsewhere for that matter. He remained his own man by keeping his own counsel. The Beezer was not given to envy. Even so, on the two occasions on which he had encountered Mrs Allison Wingfield he understood why Deacon's affair had given rise to much carping bitterness among the planters and their agents. Mrs Allison Wingfield was undoubtedly desirable. Her liaison with the handsome captain crowned Deacon's legend nicely, the more so as Deacon didn't give a damn what people thought of him.

Beasley said, 'That will be all, Jeffrey.'

'Thank you, Major.'

'Oh, one minor point . . .'

'Sir?'

'When would you estimate that Pawson will trundle in with the swag?'

'Three days, sir. Possibly four.'

'I would appreciate it if you are on hand.'

'I have to confess that I didn't try to make headway with Kwai Yan Chung. I mean, sir, that I do not have even a rudimentary relationship with him.'

'Didn't you even ask him about his chum?'

'About Shan? No, sir. I did not.'

'Why not?'

'I wouldn't give Kwai Yan Chung the satisfaction of sneering at me. Besides, I was obliged to concentrate on simply staying awake.'

'In any case, that isn't the reason I want you here for the unveiling.'

'What is the reason, Major?'

'Saunders is coming.'

'Dear God!'

'I believe you and he are acquainted.'

'Yes, we are. After a fashion.'

'I've never met the man. Best if you're on hand.'

'Of course, Major.'

'Don't mind, do you?'

'Not at all,' said Deacon, lying glibly.

Deacon was not the only officer to retain rooms in the St John's Hotel but, being wealthy, he did things in style.

The upper floor suite was permanently registered in his name. Its closets contained his clothing, its cases his books, its dressing-table held his collection of toilet articles. Servants of the management clamoured to attend *Tuan* Deacon for he was not only famous but was also a generous tipper. There were four rooms to the suite, including, as the 'jewel in the crown', the most opulent bathroom outside of the Sultan's palace. It was a masterpiece of blue and green tile with a hot tub, a cold plunge and a circular shower that, said Allison Wingfield, made one feel as if one was bathing in the heart of a marble column. Huge copper pipes and burnished Victorian fitments flushed the water up from the hotel's basement and sluiced it away again. The only flaw in the plumbing was the lurid noises that it emitted from time to time, an effect which not even money could cure or be rid of.

For the sake of 'tone', Mrs Allison Wingfield resided in an apartment on the hotel's second floor, directly below that of her close friend, Captain Jeffrey Alexander Deacon. Mrs Wingfield paid her own bills; she would have it no other way.

'I may have no shame, Jeff, but I prefer not to be a kept woman.'

Deacon understood. Since the sale of the Wade-Wingfield plantation to the Delaware Rubber Company, Mrs Allison Wingfield was independently wealthy. She did not need to be dependent on the captain for life's little luxuries. She chose to stay in the St John's, in Malaya, of her own free will. She chose to stay because of Deacon. In addition, freed from a repressive marriage by the grisly death of her husband during a guerrilla raid, she – like Deacon – had a purpose which kept her there. She too wanted to see Wei Sand Shan captured, tried and executed. It did not strike Allison as odd that the very event which had released her from bondage to her husband Clive and had brought Jeff Deacon into her life had also stoked up her hatred of the Communists. She loved Jeff Deacon, however, with a fierce and dedicated passion which increased her fear whenever he was away from her and which twined into her character a resolve that came close to courage.

During the captain's prolonged absences, Allison went about the town's social gatherings as boldly as if she was a Christian missionary, dismissive of sympathy, equally dismissive of guilt. She defended the 'shining armour' of the men of the SAS and the other British army units whose presence in Port Kernan was, strangely, resented by diehard colonials. The surprising thing was that the leaders of Port Kernan's stuffy society tolerated, even encouraged, Allison Wingfield. They did not ostracize her, did not edge her out into the cold. She was more in demand as a dinner guest than ever she had been as the wife of Clive Wingfield, a person, it was privately agreed, who was decidedly *déclassé*. Mrs Wingfield had a pedigree of her own and was 'the consort' of a member of the English Landed Gentry. She was fully entitled to her 'eccentricities'.

By a discreet financial arrangement with a junior admin clerk in Major Beasley's office, Mrs Wingfield received direct and up-to-the-hour reports on Captain Deacon's whereabouts. She asked for no details, nothing that might be classed as 'secret' information. She merely wanted to know that Jeff was safely back in the Port so that she might prepare herself for his term of leave by cancelling all other appointments.

She never knew quite what to expect. It was not that Jeff was given to moods, simply that his trips into the heartland of Malaya might be exhilarating or harrowing or depleting, and she had to prepare for each and all. His scarred body might be whittled down to skin and bone. He might have suppurating tick sores to be bathed and dressed, or a jungle rash or ugly little wounds of one sort or another. A cabinet of medicines in a corner of the luxurious bathroom was ready to meet such emergencies. Sometimes Jeff would be too exhausted to make love to her. On other occasions he would return as rampantly as a bull loosed from a pasture. Out of love, not duty, Allison would try to engage with whatever mood Jeff brought back with him, to fulfil his need of her in every possible way. He was the warrior, one of the élite. She worshipped him for his skill, his tenacity and his courage by serving him well as a mistress.

Drinks were on the table, ice in the bowl, fresh fruit in the basket. The water in the taps in the bathroom was piping hot. In the kitchens, though it was late afternoon, a chicken pilaf steamed in the oven, ready to be whisked up to the suite if the captain should wish to eat.

From the window of her bedroom, Allison watched a jeep deliver Jeff Deacon in the street outside the hotel. He carried a canvas holdall and wore the revolver holster on his belt. The jungle greens were gone, discarded at the camp, but an odd assortment of combat gear marked him and set him apart. The Canadian, Campbell, was the second passenger in the jeep.

The vehicle halted long enough for Jeff and the sergeant to talk together for a few moments. The sergeant was ebullient and waved vigorously as the jeep pulled away into the light traffic. Campbell had a girl waiting too, a Chinese girl, very young and very pretty.

Jeff came quickly across the pavement and entered under the awning of the hotel. Without further delay, Allison went up the back staircase and into the third-floor suite. A couple of minutes later, Jeff entered. He slung the holdall to the floor and removed his belt and jacket before he came to her. He touched her gently at first, as if afraid that he would bruise her. He kissed her mouth.

'How long, darling?' Allison asked.

'Three days. Possibly four.'

'Then what?'

'I'll be around for a couple of weeks at least. Saunders is coming. Number One Copper, in person.'

'I detest that man.'

'You are not alone.'

'Drink?'

'Bath,' said Deacon.

Obediently Allison entered the bathroom and drew water into the deep, oval tub. Filtered, the water was pure and clear, unlike the water in other parts of the town, which often ran brown. In the bedroom, Jeff undressed. Wearing a terrycloth robe, he came into the bathroom. He kissed her again. She began to get an impression of his mood, one of triumph. He was weary but cheerful.

She said, 'Shall I scrub your back?'

'And wet that pretty dress?'

'Shall I take it off?'

'Why not?'

Deacon turned off the bath taps and shed the robe. He stepped into the thigh-deep water, his back to her, and slid down until the water reached his chin.

Through the steam he watched Allison step out of her panties and slip the catch on her brassiere. Her body was strong, her breasts heavy. She moved, naked, without inhibitions, stepped over the rounded rim of the tub and slid down opposite him.

Deacon said, 'You look well.'

'Thank you, kind sir.'

'Did you miss me?'

'Dreadfully.'

Leaning forward, Deacon kissed her breasts, her nipples. He kissed her mouth then lay back, slopping the water in the tub. Allison moved on all fours over him and returned his kiss with interest, then found the soap, worked it into a creamy lather and began to massage his body.

Deacon said, 'You haven't asked me about the operation.'

The woman hesitated, tensing. 'Did you . . .?'

'No, not Shan. But we did capture Kwai Yan Chung.'

'Really?'

'Really!' said Deacon. 'Pawson's bringing him in now.'

'Better than nothing, I suppose.'

'Much better,' said Deacon. 'We also succeeded in taking the camp. Not too many prisoners but enough to keep Intelligence fully occupied for quite some days.'

'Is it because of Yan Chung that Saunders is deigning to visit us?' said Allison.

'Somebody is supplying Shan with money and American-made arms. It's rather unfortunate that we didn't manage to catch the little swine on the spot but we had to nobble the encampment while we could. For once, Shan was careless.'

'Is he losing his influence, do you think?'

'Not that,' said Deacon. 'A touch of over-confidence, more probably.'

'Yan Chung won't talk. He won't spill the beans.'

'Oh, he might,' said Deacon. 'You never can tell what sort of squabbling there's been between the leaders. Funny people, the CTs. Look at Mao Tan. When he was captured down in Johore, he turned his coat immediately and blabbed away nineteen to the dozen. He saved the Security Forces thousands of hours of dog labour and man-power. Nobody expected it. He was reputed to be one of the most loyal and ferocious of all the CTs in the Fifth.'

Allison resumed her massage. Her touch was firm but not yet erotic in intent. There would be time enough for that.

'Kwai Yan Chung might also be rather interested in saving his neck,' said Deacon. 'I wouldn't be surprised if that's why Saunders is coming; to offer some sort of deal, an amnesty in exchange for hard core information. Saunders is almost as keen to take Wei Sand Shan as we are.'

'Yes,' the woman said, 'but for Saunders it's a matter of furthering his career, enhancing his reputation.'

'True, he's an egotistical swine but he is good at his job.'

'Did you lose anyone?'

'One or two wounded in mopping up. We got off with hardly a scratch.'

'Intact?'

Deacon smiled. 'That part of me is intact.'

'So I see.'

Shifting his hips, Deacon adjusted his position to demonstrate a change in interest. Clearly he was no longer keen to talk shop. Her breasts swung before him. He stroked and fondled them softly then drew her down upon him, clasping her with his thighs.

Tenderness and sexual hunger washed over him. He felt the

soft wetness of her envelop him, her breasts crush against his chest, her hair against his cheek. He lifted himself again and entered her, not with excessive urgency but with a sensation of relief, of luxury, different from that which he had known with other women. But this was only a part of it, though an important part, an aspect of their affair which did not dominate. Later, after he had rested and they had dined together and returned to the room, he would lie with her on the bed under the cool, clicking blades of the fan and they would talk, touch and talk, and it would be love-making of another kind, no less satisfying, no less intimate than what they did in and against the bathtub.

Tonight he would tell her the good news, that at the end of his tour, in eight months time, he planned to resign his commission and return to England with her.

Provided, of course, that Wei Sand Shan was dead.

A full round moon stood over the sea. It silhouetted the palm trees which fringed the beach of the Paradise Gardens. Strings of coloured lanterns hung motionless. The air was balmy. From the dance deck, under a pagoda roof, you could just make out creamy waves curling on the sand and the glitter of moonlight far out where breakers leapt ceaselessly over the reef of Pulau Kemask. What you could not see, because Mr Hauser had so arranged it, was the chain-link fence which protected the beach and the ten-acre garden. Even in daylight the defences were not obvious, the scruffy red tennis court and the swimming-pool screened by banks of flowering shrubs. But every soldier, flyer and marine commando who frequented the Paradise Gardens was aware of the fence and felt secure because of it.

The Paradise had become a country club for 'other ranks'. It was one place in Port Kernan where a man could forget jungles and swamps, shake off the weight of combat packs and guns. Here he could relax with a girl, drink cold beer or Highland Park, or feed his face at the hotel's hot-and-cold buffet tables.

Mr Hauser, a German-born émigré, had owned the old Paradise Beach House for many years. During Hitler's war he had faced ruin because of it. He had served the 'visiting' Japanese with a reluctance that amounted to hostility, let the gardens and the buildings run to seed while he got on with spying for the Allied Intelligence Services, tapping out nightly messages on the state of shipping in the Strait or troop movements on Bay Boulevard.

God or circumstance had rewarded Mr Hauser for his loyalty to the British. With the advent of Allied forces in Malaya and the establishment of the SAS post only a half-mile away, business boomed. Now Mr Hauser was on his way to minting a fortune.

Mr Hauser was a benign little man who, after thirty-six years in South-east Asia, looked more Malayan than most Malays. He wore a white evening-jacket and a plaid sarong beneath whose hem a pair of patent-leather dancing pumps gleamed. Mr Hauser was affable without being effusive. He was not much in evidence around the dance deck or in the open bars. Mr Hauser had four or five 'wives', all past their prime, and a brood of sons and daughters, many of whom had gone into the entertainment business on their own account, in Penang, KL and Singapore.

Beneath its semi-respectable surface, of course, the Paradise was not much more than a glorified knocking-shop. But its girls were clean, decent and trustworthy, beer was never watered and prices not much inflated. In addition Mr Hauser had his own methods of subduing brawlers. They were dealt with by two 'bandsmen' who just happened to be trained in the art of Thai boxing. It was a humiliating experience to be knocked out by a bare-footed second violinist, to waken in the cold room behind the kitchens, where Mr Hauser would hand you a cup of scalding hot coffee with one hand and a bill for breakages with the other. But it was better than being turned over to the MPs or the local police. Even the roughest soldiers complied with the Paradise Gardens' unwritten rules of behaviour.

Susu Mafan lived in style in one of the thatch cabins which hugged the fence on the harbour side. Though Buz Campbell was a generous guy he did not pay the girl's rent. He went along with Mr Hauser's suggestion that the girl be allowed to work for it by cleaning. Secretly, Buz resented the fact that his 'lady' spent so much time on her knees with a scrub brush. But he was in no position just yet to set her up in style. He agreed with Hauser that it was better she have something to do with her time while he, Buz, was up-country. Buz trusted Mr Hauser to keep Susu on the straight and narrow, to see to it that she didn't take up with passing trade. It wasn't that the girl was wicked or greedy but she was young, susceptible to flattery, and liked 'bed tricks' very much indeed.

Times, Buz thought he was crazy to sustain the relationship. Other times it made him feel wonderful. He would look at Susu while she sat on the stool by the dressing-table in the cabin, the bakelite radio crooning by her side and all her little paint pots laid out, and wonder what she saw in him, apart from 'sugar'. He would experience twinges of guilt, and the oppression of all his years in uniform would weigh heavily on him. And she would come to him, sit on his knees and offer her breast to him, like a gift. And he would stop feeling bad and start feeling like a young stud without a goddamned care in the world. Only ramrod NCOs, those with creases ironed into their pyjamas and photographs of fat wives and spotty kids on their lockers, despised Buz Campbell for taking his share of honey. Most guys figured the old bastard had it made. They envied him.

It was not hard to like little Susu Mafan. Even P.B. tolerated her, though he missed the companionship of his hard-drinking buddy and privately believed that the kid would bring grief in the long run. When Buz growled about quitting the SAS and settling down with Susu on some little paddi farm on one of the remote estates, P.B. made non-committal noises. Even if old Buz imagined he might be happy as a simple dirt farmer, P.B. couldn't see the kid putting up with it for long. Susu was young enough to crave bright lights and a fast pace. P.B. couldn't fathom why she had drifted into staid Port Kernan, unless it was in pursuit of a meal-ticket like Buz. But then P.B. would be the first to admit that he didn't understand women, whatever their age, colour or creed. Now and then, P.B. would be tempted to take up Susu's kindly offer to find him a 'lady' too. But it never quite worked out and he spent his nights, even his leaves, tucked up in barracks.

P.B. merely endured his spells in Port Kernan, waiting to get back on patrol, back into the jungle, closer to the possibility of a scrap. Buz no longer had the stomach for it and his heart stayed home in the Paradise Gardens. Things might have gone on like this for months, even years, if it hadn't been for the taking of Kwai Yan Chung and the events which followed his arrest. Deacon saw none of it. P.B. McNair and Buz Campbell, however, had grandstand seats for the show.

The Paradise Gardens was chock-full that Wednesday night. Pawson's boys, who had trooped in from the jungle early that day, were out to celebrate. The place was alive with jollity. Toasts to Kwai Yan Chung and the guys of 'K' Squadron who had captured the fat bastard were drunk at every table. Nabbing the second most wanted bandit in the North was an event worthy of celebration. Nineteen prisoners were tucked away safe and sound. Eleven were in hospital. Eight, including Kwai Yan Chung, were locked in the town jail.

There should have been more prisoners but the delay between the bombing and the arrival of the back-up unit had let many off the hook. The body count was impressive as hell, though. Ninety-three dead. Ninety-three CTs less to worry about. The stuffing was knocked out of Sand Shan's guerrilla army in the north states. Nobody could calculate how many innocent lives had been saved by the operation, and its propaganda value was incredibly high. As far as the SAS were concerned, it was a little more than an ordinary 'day's work'. They felt entitled to let their hair down before the Beezer summoned them to heel and reminded them that there was still much to be done before the Red Menace was swept from the Peninsula for ever.

By nine-thirty, P.B. was half-seas-over, and enjoying himself no end. He was seated at a big, white-painted, iron table, surrounded by younger and more impressionable soldiers. Beer bottles and dishes of rice and seafood which had been demolished by the troops, littered the table. Johnny Badhur was absent. The Gurkha had no liking for the Gardens. He would probably be with his regimental cronies in the cocktail lounge of the Greenhall Rest House, or playing squash on the town's only court. Where the redoubtable Dyak, Umgah, had sneaked off to in search of rest and relaxation was anybody's guess. Idly, heavy-lidded, P.B. watched Buz and the girl on the dance-floor. No doubt about it, Susu was the best-looking lassie in the place. There were thirty or so couples weaving on the teak-wood dance deck. If you were half-cut and sleepy and not too bloody discriminating, you could fancy it was romantic. But most of the punters were after one thing. Soft talk and cuddling would be a prelude to bartering about price.

Buz was near twice as tall as Susu. She had her head laid against his breastbone while they shuffled about the floor. Buz's hands were draped over her shoulders. She hugged his thickening waist. P.B. could see the kid's face slanted against the glow of the lanterns, sloped eyes half-closed. He wondered in a vague sort of way what was on her mind, what she was dreaming about. He could guess what old Buz was dreaming about. If it wasn't bed in the thatched hut, it would be a paddi farm far from uniforms and the reek of spilled beer.

'So now we got the bastard, P.B., what yer fink we'll do wiff 'im?'

'God knows!'

''Ang 'im up by the balls 'til 'e squawks.'

'Yer, 'anging's too bleedin' good for 'im.'

'He'll talk. I hear Saunders is on his way.'

'Saunders? Bleedin' 'ell.'

'Be 'ere termorrer, I 'eard.'

'Saunders'll make the Chink talk, double bloody quick.'

P.B. said, 'We'll all b' back on patrol come Saturday.'

'Nuffin' ter patrol now. We got all the big bleeders under lock'n' key.'

'Don't you believe it, son,' said P.B.

'Plenty more for you yet, Fred.'

'Nah! Sand Shan's finished.'

'Ever seen him?' P.B. asked.

'Can't say I ever 'ad the pleasure.'

'You seen 'im, P.B.?'

'Aye, sure. On the Wingfield dust-up.'

'What's 'e look like, like?'

'Like Lord fuckin' Snooty wi' glasses.'

'Yer kiddin'.'

'Butter wouldnae melt in his mouth.'

'Did 'e really shop the Deke?'

P.B. would not discuss the private affairs of his commander in the field. He knew little of Deacon's experiences at the hands of the Japanese, only that Deacon and Shan had been on a deep cover operation together in 1945 and that Shan had sold Deacon out. Now the Deke had it in for Sand Shan, wouldn't be at peace until the rebel leader was dead or imprisoned. P.B. understood the nature of vengeance. It was simple enough to require no explanations, a good clean reason for fighting.

The corporal said, 'How'd I know?'

'You been with the Deke longer'n anybody, P.B.'

'Aye. Way back. In the desert. Way back, afore there was a Special Air Service.'

'So what was 'e like, like?'

P.B. shrugged and reached for the bottle of Highland Park which stood among the litter of glasses on the iron table.

It was a bizarre moment.

The dance deck, the band of Malayan musicians in their alcove, mellow light on brass saxophones and trumpets, the smootchy sounds of the dance tune. Palms. Waves on the beach. Buz and the young Chinese girl hugging and swaying under the lanterns. The eager, sweating faces of the warriors around him.

The spot of colour was like an orchid blooming suddenly in the dark, salty shrubs.

Fire.

P.B. stretched out his arms. He grabbed the edges of the round table. He rolled over backwards, bringing the table and its contents over on him and three or four of his companions. White, wet iron came up like a shield.

Bullets tore into the trellis behind him. He heard the ringing metallic whine of bullets on the table itself. He squirmed, slithering left. He shouted at the pitch of his voice. The warning came too late, of course, far too late.

The attack lasted no longer than a couple of minutes. It was brief, bloody and merciless. The bandstand went up in splinters. Strings of lanterns whipped away on the blast, darkening the scene after the one brilliant flash which rolled up the teak-wood deck like a hearthrug and shook it out all over the garden.

There was no attempt at follow-up. Submachine-guns, trained inwards on the soldiers, discharged over a thousand rounds into the crowd.

'Buz? Jesus! Buz?' P. B. McNair shouted as he crawled towards the wreckage of the dance-floor.

Buz Campbell didn't answer him.

Buz lay on the gravel, twenty feet from the place where the deck had been. He was winded, stunned and shocked. In his arms he held the headless body of little Susu Mafan.

Deacon was drinking coffee at the end of dinner in the dining-room of the St John's Hotel when a shock wave quivered through the room. Glass and crystal tinkled.

The diners stiffened.

Deacon wasn't the only officer in the St John's but he was first to his feet and first out of the room. He went up the stairs three at a time and down them again in great leaps with the Browning automatic in his hand. He still wore his dinner-suit and polished shoes. He came down between the potted plants and across the foyer just in time to catch the second explosion. The long, low, sinister rumble of high explosive came, he judged, from the western end of the port. Allison had emerged from the dining-room, together with six army officers and an RAF Pilot Officer, followed by waiters and women.

Deacon snapped out orders. 'Spinks, will you escort the ladies away from the doors and windows? Take them to the cellar.'

'What is it, Jeff? What's happened, do you think?'

'Richard, Peter, come with me. Keep alert, all of you.' Deacon touched Allison's arm. 'Go with the lieutenant, darling, please.'

'Take care, Jeff.'

'I will,' Deacon promised.

The door of the hotel opened. Deacon braced his right wrist with his left hand and pivoted towards the couple who entered. It was an elderly planter and his younger wife, known to Deacon by sight.

'What the deuce . . .?' the planter spluttered.

'My apologies,' said Deacon. 'What's happening in the street?'

'Damned bombs goin' off everywhere.'

'Where?'

'Appears to be the damned Gardens . . . and the hospital—'

'And the gaol?' Deacon asked.

'Matter of fact, yes.'

'Where's your car, sir?'

'Boy's puttin' it away.'

'Richard?'

'Rightio,' said Lieutenant Richard Forest.

'Gentlemen,' Deacon said, 'the town appears to be under attack from CTs. Make your way back to base with extreme caution. We can't do much without weapons.'

Forest returned. 'Car, Jeff.'

'With your permission, sir?' said Deacon to the planter.

'What? What?'

'Take it, of course,' said the planter's wife.

Deacon hurried out of the St John's Hotel with his brother officers.

The sky to the north was blanched with soft, wavering light. Closer, blocked by the glazed stone of the Portuguese church, there was smoke. It looked fake, as if somebody had sketched it with chalk against the night sky. Street lamps showed the shadows of pedestrians and bicyclists pressed against the walls. The chatter of gunfire was faint but audible in the wide boulevard to the right of the St John's.

Forest had already taken the wheel of the car, a Chevrolet sedan. Peter Rees was crouched by the passenger door.

Rees shouted, 'Which way, Deke?'

Leaning on the car's armoured roof, Deacon scanned the skyline above the buildings. 'The gaol,' he decided, and dropped into the leather seat beside Forest.

The car's powerful engine revved. The vehicle shot forward. Swerving into a U-turn, with Forest expertly fisting the wheel, it stood practically on its running-board as it swung around a horse-island.

The clanging of the old-fashioned bell on the bracket of the Port Kernan fire engine burst through the snarl of the Chevrolet's four-litre engine. Forest braked, stamped on the accelerator and powered the car past the tail-board of the fire engine. Deacon glimpsed the startled brown features of the Malay firemen, then grabbed the dash as the Chevrolet flung right again and, with clearway ahead, tooled up to eight mph.

Two jeeps showed ahead, under the wan street-lamps.

'Police?' shouted Forest.

'Don't risk it,' shouted Deacon.

The Chevrolet's windshield was of thick, plated glass, compressed by surrounds of inch-thick steel. It was like riding in a tank, only tanks seldom travelled at more than a mile a minute. The jeeps were not the black-and-white painted jobs that the Port Kernan Police Force used for urban patrols.

'Bandits!'

A hail of bullets streaked around the Chevrolet. They shuddered off the plating and thumb-printed the glass in front of Deacon's nose. He flinched and ducked, in spite of himself. The car flashed past the parked jeeps and took the bullets broadside down its doors and wings.

'God in Heaven!' Rees exclaimed loudly, from the rear seat.

'It's the gaol,' said Forest. 'They're raiding the gaol.'

'They must be springing Kwai Yan Chung, the impudent beggars. Where are the police?' said Rees, leaning over the padded seat.

'Elsewhere,' said Deacon. 'It's a three-prong attack at least. Diversions everywhere.'

'Lucky we're here,' said Forest.

'Isn't it?' said Deacon.

'I hope this car's insured,' said Rees.

Forest swung round a monument, a grotesque, Edwardian bronze of The Spirit of Commerce. He brought the Chevrolet back along the kerbside.

The gaol was a low building of two storeys, set behind walls and palms. The gates had been blown open. The candy-striped guard-box was on fire, a casual flicker of burning wood. They glimpsed a sprawled figure in the uniform of the Malayan Special Police. There was the sound of gunfire from behind the hooded palms. Lights blazed in the upper storey of the building.

'Now where . . .?' said Forest, peering.

The jeeps had vanished.

'Damn me, they've gone inside,' said Rees.

'Lunatics,' said Forest.

He braked and brought the Chevrolet to a halt fifty yards from the gate. He glanced at Deacon.

'After them?'

'Does anybody know what's at the rear?' Deacon enquired.

'Exercise yard, kitchens, that sort of thing.'

'An exit?'

'Not for transport.'

'In that case,' said Deacon, 'stick this armour-plated monster across the gate.'

Forest laughed. 'Wizard!'

He rolled the Chevrolet on to the pavement and crawled it alongside the wall.

Rees said, 'I assume, old chappies, that we're not going to sit tight and have a little puff until the banditos re-appear?'

The sedan came gently to rest directly in front of the open gates of the gaol. The three SAS officers peered from the windows down the avenue between ornamental palm trees at the building beyond. The noise of gunfire had ceased. There were no signs at all of the two CT jeeps.

'Going in?' asked Rees.

'Unarmed?' said Deacon. 'I'm the only one with a gun.'

'Oh, we'll find something to shoot.'

Rees and Deacon climbed from the Chevrolet. Forest tugged on the handbrake and withdrew the ignition key and joined them against the wall. The huge American sedan, weighted with steel, blocked the gate most effectively.

'What if somebody wants in, our chaps, say?'

'Hide yourself,' said Deacon. 'Find a gun if you can. Should be something near the guard-box.'

'What are you going to do?'

'Nose about. There's something horribly fishy about this situation.'

'A masterpiece of understatement, Deke.'

Leaving Rees and Forest behind, Deacon stole forward down the line of palms which fringed the avenue to the main building.

It had been built in the days when 'Leeds Gothic' was all the rage in colonial towns. It looked like a town hall with a couple of tiers removed. Around the roof were gun emplacements disguised by a stonework balustrade, defence against rioters and peasant uprisings which had never been used in peaceful Port Kernan.

Deacon had no weapon except the automatic pistol. He still wore his dinner-suit. He was perspiring profusely by now but had lost the initial sense of excitement, the sixth sense which told him when danger was imminent.

The gaol and the adjacent police depot seemed to be deserted. At the top of six broad stone steps the front door exposed an empty foyer. Deacon kneeled by the base of the last palm. Forty yards of open square lay between him and the door. If the CTs were hidden in the trees, and he made a bolt for it . . .

Decision was rendered unnecessary. From the doorway of the main building came three Malay constables, booted, hatted and clutching rifles. A fourth followed, limping. He had a pistol on a lanyard. They dipped from the doorway and threw themselves down upon the steps, rifles pointing outwards in

Deacon's direction. From an upstairs window, to Deacon's left, a high-pitched voice yelled something which Deacon could not interpret. The wounded constable fired the pistol, without aim, into the palms.

Deacon faded behind the tree bole.

He could not understand it. The Port Kernan Police Division was a tough, well-drilled force, yet they were firing at ghosts.

Rifles cracked. Bullets whirred in the palm fronds. Deacon got down low and sneaked a glance at the doorway. More policemen had appeared, bottled in the tiled foyer. On the rooftop too there were shapes. Rifles. Whispered cries. But no sign of the jeeps. No trace of a bandit. If Rees hadn't seen the jeeps turn into the grounds, Deacon would have been inclined to believe that he had been in error, that the bandits had made good their escape.

He put his hand to his mouth and shouted in English. 'Don't shoot. I'm Captain Deacon, "K" Squadron, SAS.'

The policemen were not that rattled by the events of the night. Nobody fired.

A voice called out, 'Where are your men?'

'I have no men. Two at the gate, only. I'm about to show myself. For God's sake, don't shoot.'

Nervously, Deacon stepped from the shelter of the trees.

'I recognize you, Captain. Come forward.'

Deacon walked quickly to the stone steps.

The Malayan sergeant said, 'There is nobody outside?'

'Two jeeps. They came in here.'

'It is not a good business, Captain.'

'What happened?'

'Ten guerrillas. They came without warning. They stormed the constables' room—'

'Kwai Yan Chung, did they take him?'

'All prisoners.'

'Where are they?' said Deacon. 'Where the devil are they?'

At that moment a constable brought Deacon an answer. He was a young man, hardly more than a boy. Perhaps this was his first taste of action. He came haring through the corridors of the building, boots clacking on the wooden flooring. He flung himself through the crowd of policemen by the door. He babbled out his account in Malayan.

Before the boy finished, Deacon shouted, 'You four, come with me.'

He went down the side of the parade-ground into the narrow avenue by the side of the building, running hard.

Stealth was not needed now, not if what the constable had said was half-way true. From behind the wall, Deacon caught the wail of a Security Patrol's siren, the clangour of an ambulance. Everything seemed fragmented, incidents weirdly isolated in this almost empty compound under the English architecture.

Unseen English voices bellowed orders.

'McArthur, take the Pitt Street end. Redfern, the Harbour Road.'

An army detail had obviously been summoned by telephone from within police headquarters. Deacon kept on running, the armed Malayan constables behind him running with a high lift of the knees, their rifles at the port.

Deacon came around the gable and into the yard at the rear just as a group of policemen debouched from the two screened doors. Deacon had been prepared to open fire with the automatic pistol. But he had no need to waste bullets.

Both jeeps had been abandoned. They had been drawn neatly into a flank on each side of the wrought-iron gate, a 'tradesman's entrance' which had been blown off its hinges and hung askew, sprouting strands of barbed wire like tree creepers. Beyond the gate lay the rump of the harbour district. Crowded bungalows packed into four narrow streets behind stone-built shipping offices which commanded a view of the quays of the port and lading docks.

Deacon slowed to a walk. The constables fell in behind him.

The purpose of that odd arrangement of the jeeps became clear. It was not to guide the escaping prisoners into the road to freedom. It was to prevent them ducking away. It wasn't an escape but an execution.

Each of the prisoners had been shot in the back. Those who had not died at once had had a bullet put through their skulls at close range.

Like a whale stranded out of water, Kwai Yan Chung lay on his belly with his arms by his sides, head twisted to one side. His eyes were open. His tongue protruded. Blood trickled stickily from his mouth. He still wore the clothing which marked him as a terrorist, the stained jungle rig in which he had been brought to Port Kernan earlier that day. The authorities hadn't even had time to 'process' him.

A Malayan police sergeant came up by Deacon's side.

'How did this happen? We did not shoot at them.'

'I know,' said Deacon.

'My instructions were to keep the prisoners alive at all costs.'

'They were dispatched by their own people,' said Deacon.

'The devils!'

'It's an irony,' said Deacon, 'really it is.'

'Sir?'

'This is obviously the work of one of Kwai Yan Chung's killer squads. A wonderful job they made of it, too.'

The sergeant gave a little grunt of displeasure. 'Where are the killers now, however?'

'Oh, they'll be well away,' said Deacon. 'But I suggest you marshall your forces so that you may be ready for a search of the harbour area when your officer gets here.'

'A fine idea, Captain,' said the sergeant. 'What of the corpses?'

'Leave them exactly as they are,' said Deacon. 'This is one photograph I do want to see plastered on the front page of every newspaper in Asia.'

Deacon got to his feet. He gave one last glance at the dead communist. Number Two on the Wanted List. Massacred by Number One. Deacon had no doubt at all who had ordered the murders: Sand Shan.

Murder by demand was exactly Shan's style.

Turning on his heel, Deacon strode from the scene to find his brother officers and hitch a ride back to the garrison to discover what other crimes had been committed in the Port that night.

Blood dappled the front of Buz Campbell's beach shirt and the fly of his duck pants. His face was drawn and his eyes hollow.

'Wee man,' he said, 'you got any cash-money on you?'

'Aye.' P.B. dug into the pocket of his shirt. 'Fifty or sixty dollars.'

'Make me a loan.'

'Sure thing, Buz.'

Buz took the roll of Malayan notes and added it to the wad in his fist. He fanned it out carefully on the desk of the nursing station and, licking the ball of his thumb, counted it.

'A hundred and ten bucks,' he said.

'Buz?'

'Come on.'

'Where're we goin'?'

'Things to do.'

'But . . .'

'Can't help the kid now, wee man.'

'You're right. You're right.'

The sergeant headed out of the admission area. Nobody paid him the slightest attention. He was bruised and ached but had no injuries. The girl's body had collected the fragments and absorbed much of the blast. Another bar of the dance-hall tune and he would have shuffled round. She would have been protected by him. She would have been alive and he would have been lying on the slab in the morgue downstairs with his head held to his body by four large, catgut stitches. Crude but expedient. The living were much more important than the dead.

The hospital itself had been attacked. Out on the wing, where the CT wounded had been housed under guard, there had been a bomb attack followed by a raid by ten armed guerrillas. A goddamned killer squad. He could figure the reason for that one. Keep the gooks from blabbing. Dead men tell no tales, right? But the raid on the Paradise Gardens had been a bloody, merciless diversion, intended to kill and maim, to create an extra piece of havoc to keep coppers and soldiers busy.

Buz strode out of the hospital, past the ambulances.

It had impinged upon him, entered his consciousness, that five nurses had been killed here, and one white doctor – Jamieson, an elderly Scottish surgeon. But he couldn't feel it, feel sorrow or outrage for them. He was holding himself together by concentrating on the things he had to do to get back, free and clear, to the unit.

'You okay, Buz?'

'Yeah! Yeah!'

Walking fast, the sergeant cleared the gate. P.B. trotted at his heels.

'Buz, we should be gettin' back to camp.'

'Soon, wee man.'

P.B. asked no more questions, made no more suggestions. His buddy was hurting sore.

He understood how Buz would combat it, how he would clear the decks and become a soldier once more, heart and head and guts all in it. The wee lass had never been for him anyway. Even so, the blood-red full stop that had been planted at the end of the affair would leave Buz with a bitter after-taste of hatred and despair. P.B. could not rationalize it any more than Buz. But there were things that were best kept separate from soldiering, from fighting and killing. Buz wouldn't find relief easy to come by.

They walked for a mile or more down narrowing streets. Leboh Ampang was the Chinese quarter where army patrols made discreet back-door 'visits' on suspected gun runners or CT suppliers, usually without much luck. Chinese Malays controlled the small boat fishing and served as merchants to the fishermen and their families. The bright, cupboard-sized shops and the awninged arcades were no tourist trap but a functioning community in their own right. The district was an oblong of crowded dwellings, padlocked warehouses, food shops and snackeries and weird one-apartment ancillary trades, like apothecaries, acupuncturists and 'drug charm' sellers. The neighbourhood stank to high heaven, not because of the Chinese Malays but because of the gnarled beach which trapped rotting fish from nets and trawl-holds.

It surprised P.B. that Buz could find his way in this quarter. He had been down here only a couple of times. It was a dangerous neighbourhood for soldiers. But Buz had had the girl behind him. Sweet little Susu, maybe she had brought him here, safe with her. Tonight, though, they were as safe as they would ever be. In the low, sweaty dwellings the Chinese would be keeping their heads down. They would know by now that there had been much trouble in the Port and that every slant-eyed one among them would be under suspicion.

Buz suddenly stopped.

The street was a jumble of wood and bamboo and glass.

The shop looked like it had been carpentered out of old fish boxes. The garish signs of the day were gone. The window had boards nailed over it, except for one square of glass the colour of a faded opal. No lights were visible within.

Buz lifted his fist and thumped it on the door. He waited impatiently, shifting his weight from one foot to the other, scowling, then he rapped again, with all the force of his arm. The building seemed to shake. The panel of opal glass rattled in its frame. Still P.B. kept his mouth shut. He wished he had had the foresight to bring along a hand-gun.

From one of the houses came the crying of a child. Far down the quays a dog was yapping. Lantern light swam within the shop. A bolt clicked on the rear of the wooden door and a wizened little face, pure Chink, peeped through the crack. In a low voice, without heat, Buz muttered a few words in a Chinese dialect. The little man bowed and vanished. A moment later the door opened. Buz stooped through into the shop. P.B. hesitantly trailed him.

P.B. didn't know what to expect.

There wasn't much in the shop to give him a clue. A belly-high counter of mahogany, without ornaments, backed on to a brown curtain. On polished brass bosses on the inner wall were cloth bolts, not shoddy, not bright, but bleached and unbleached linens and cheaper cottons. The Chinaman was old. He dressed like something out of a Charlie Chan picture, with round hat and loose robe. He even had drooping whiskers and a pigtail of sorts. He had stationed himself behind the counter and stood there with his hands hidden in the sleeves of his robe. P.B. almost expected to hear a gong ring.

Buz took the wad of dollar notes from his shirt pocket and placed it on the counter. The Chinaman's features wrinkled some more. Smiling maybe.

'You understand English?' Buz asked.

'I do, soldier.'

'All right. Down payment. Plenty more tomorrow.'

'Bank cheques, okay.'

'Yeah,' said Buz. 'Listen. There's a girl up in the hospital. She's dead. I want you to bury her. Do what you have to do. You do it all. Go fetch her. See to it that she has all the trimmings. All the bells an' stuff. Right?

The Chinaman bowed.

P.B. felt a strange constriction in his throat, a thickening of sorrow. Buz knew that he would be up-country again and wanted to come back to a clean slate.

Before he returned to the camp it would be all over. He would have closed the episode in his life labelled 'Susu Mafan' and would not be obliged to open it again. With luck the SAS might be posted on patrol for two or three months. God knows what the results of tonight's attack would be, what the high brass would order the Beezer to do about it. If it was left to the Deke, there would be no rest until Shan was found, which suited Buz just fine.

The sergeant said, 'You need authorisation?'

'I am known to the hospital people,' said the Chinaman.

'I want it done right.'

'It will be fine, dandy.'

'I don't even know what she was. Buddhist, I reckon. Some kinda Buddhist.'

'I will attend,' said the old man and, with another bow, discreetly pocketed the roll of dollar bills. 'The girl has no relatives who have need to be informed?'

Buz shook his head. 'No relatives.'

But the sergeant, in this case, was wrong.

It was half-way through the night before the Beezer called a briefing. There had been no sleep for any of his officers and the armoury and mess blazed with light. The perimeter of the camp had been stiffened with extra guards. A detail of eight men had been sent offshore in the police launch to comb known landing spots, of which there were dozens, up the coast. The SAS officers came to the meeting in the low room behind the Beezer's offices in jungle kit and bearing arms. They were ready to move out as soon as they were given instruction. To a man they smouldered with rage and indignation.

Major Beasley took the platform in front of the blackboard. He faced the men, who were seated on benches under the dim electric lights, faces shiny with sweat.

The Beezer said, 'By now you will have heard, gentlemen, that raids were carried out earlier tonight on three locations within the town. A bomb and bullet attack was made on the Paradise Gardens at approximately 21.45 hours. The object of this raid was, it seems, to tie up military and civil personnel and to divert attention and ancillary services from the principal targets which were, as we now know, the hospital and the gaol.'

On the blackboard in white chalk the Beezer drew four rectangles, one of which, scribbled with barbed wire, represented the camp. Eight lines indicated the streets of Port Kernan and an undulating line the edge of the sea.

The Beezer went on, 'We cannot yet be sure how many guerrillas were involved in each phase of the raid but it seems that the squads were small in number and exceedingly well-trained. From information that has come our way in the past months, we know that Kwai Yan Chung was the organiser and programme instructor of so-called 'killer squads'. It is reasonable to assume that the CT units employed tonight were trained by the said Kwai Yan Chung. Hoist, one might say, by his own petard.'

'Serves the bastard right,' growled a young lieutenant.

'Unfortunately Kwai Yan Chung was not the only victim,' said the Beezer. 'It is beyond doubt that the intention of the raiders was not to free the prisoners but to silence them at all costs.'

Tim Dalinart entered the room. He apologized and stepped to the platform. He handed two sheets of signals papers to the Major and then took his seat in the front row.

The Beezer glanced at the papers and wrinkled his nose.

'Preliminary investigations indicate,' the CO continued, 'that three guerrilla units entered the town separately. Two came by sea. How, we can't yet say for sure.'

Deacon put in, 'Possibly by ocean boards.'

'Silently through the surf?' mused the Beezer.

'Shan learned the technique from the SBS during the Japanese war.'

The Beezer nodded. 'It would certainly account for the fact that the security at the Paradise Gardens was breached with such ease.' He glanced at the roughly-drawn plan on the board. 'The squad which attacked the hospital came in by boat. More conventionally. By fishing-craft into the harbour. They were seen but not recognized at the time.'

'How in God's name did they get past the guards at the hospital?' Pawson asked.

'Through the staff quarters. Shooting all the way. Two CTs were shot dead. None were wounded, alas.'

'Did they get what they came for?' asked Johnny Badhur.

'They dispatched the wounded that we brought in from the Totan this morning, if that's what you mean. Very thoroughly. Shot them all.' The Beezer made more lines on the blackboard. 'Came this way. Departed by the same route, as far as we are able to deduce. It was exceedingly well planned and executed. The attack on the hospital began five minutes or less after the bombs went off in the Paradise Gardens, by which time the hospital special service units, and the guards, had much to occupy them.'

Badhur said, 'How did they reach the gaol, sir?'

'Ah, yes. They "removed" the guard post on the B-grade road below the junction with the Australian Plantation. Four dead and two seriously wounded. They came down by jeep from there and rode boldly up to the hospital.'

'Why didn't they take the jeeps inside straight away?' asked Spinks. 'Isn't that puzzling, sir?'

The Beezer said, 'Captain Deacon suggests that the jeeps were also a diversion and that they, the main party, entered the gaol through the rear gate. Who can say, at this stage? The important thing is that they were disturbed by three of our officers. It doesn't seem to have hindered them much, one way or the other. The prisoners were broken out of the cells on the first and second blocks, which are both on ground level. Resistance from the police night-duty detail was held off by a splinter group. It really was, I must say, a very sophisticated manoeuvre for the communists.'

'What was the death toll, sir?' asked Pawson.

'High,' said Beasley. 'Too high. Murderously high. We've been injured, gentlemen. We've been insulted, too, if you take my meaning. The bandits out-foxed us. They moved much more quickly than we had reason to expect they would. They did not muck about with retributions and reprisals for our recent success in cutting off their column and destroying the training base at the Totan. All of which seems a shade pale, I'm afraid to say.'

Pawson persisted, 'What are we going to do about tonight, Major?'

The Beezer studied the map again. He shook the signals messages slightly, as if watering the heads of the officers nearest him. 'For the moment – nothing.'

Deacon grunted. It was much as he had expected. He could see sense in it. But one or two of the less seasoned officers were up in arms, full of spleen and resentment. They protested loudly until the Beezer shouted for order and gained sullen silence.

'I have been *ordered* to do nothing here,' the major explained. 'I am to attend a meeting of all services in Singapore the day after tomorrow. In the meantime, we will tighten our security, double the guards, and continue with scheduled patrols. That, gentlemen, is all.'

Deacon said, 'Shan will go to ground, sir.'

'Of course he will,' said the Beezer. 'Oh, don't mistake me. I'd much prefer it if we marshalled and dispatched all our teams at first light tomorrow. I'm sure you and your chaps would be only too happy to get on the track of this menace. But we must tread with care and due caution for a bit. Contain ourselves.'

'Until when, sir?' asked Spinks.

'Until we have a lead,' said Tim Dalinart.

'And until I find out what alteration in policy this dirty business might occasion,' said the Beezer. 'Be assured I won't have my bottom kicked for this one, gentlemen, and I won't come back from Singapore empty-handed.'

'Now what the hell does he mean by that?' murmured Forest.

Deacon answered, 'He means there will be a campaign.'

'I thought there was already,' said Forest.

'Listen,' Deacon advised.

Major Beasley went on, 'The Commissioner's reluctance to employ force against the Chinese civilian population is understandable, but I'm not at all sure that a certain "rooting out", shall we say, of communist supporters is not now essential. The gloves must come off. The communists aren't like us. They do not play by our rules. We will have to accept that fact, however unpalatable it is. Russia and China might condone the tactics that Shan and his gangsters employ, but our moral standpoint is not that of our enemy.'

'Christ, I wish he'd stop,' whispered Spinks. 'I just want to get out there and hammer the bastards into the dirt.'

'Easy,' said Deacon. 'I think he's telling us that we must not be rushed into hasty actions at this particular stage.'

The Beezer gave his officers a hard stare.

'Emergency conditions and full alert status will prevail, of course,' he said. 'As soon as we have a clue as to where Shan has gone to ground then we'll mount a massive inter-service operation . . .'

'Another operation,' said Forest. 'He's mad about operations.'

'. . . to make sure that this time we do trap him.'

'Sir,' said Tim Dalinart, 'how long is that liable to take?'

'I can't say.'

'Weeks, sir, or months?'

There was no love lost between Dalinart and Beasley. The adjutant was putting in the tip of his boot. Every man there realised it – except the Beezer.

The major puffed out his cheeks.

'Depends on Intelligence, as you know, Tim.'

'And luck, sir?'

'Luck?' said the Beezer. 'No such thing.'

'You want me to wait outside, Buz?' said P.B. McNair.

'Nope. Come on in.'

P.B. followed Buz into the bungalow which was no more than a glorified beach cabin, complete with geckoes on the ceiling and ants around the wainscot. It was stiflingly hot inside; Buz had neglected to switch on the fan. Cheap furniture. Big double bed with a wicker headboard, a couple of wicker chairs, a plywood wardrobe and dressing-table. To P.B. it seemed that the room's one purpose was to provide privacy. But the presence of the girl, like an amiable spirit, lingered. A whiff of cheap perfume, oddments of jewellery on a tortoiseshell tray on the dressing-table top.

Buz switched on a paper-shaded lamp. He looked around. His features, heavy as dough, were without expression. He picked up a nylon nightdress from the foot of the bed and crumpled it into a ball.

'Gimme a bag, wee man.'

P.B. glanced round.

'In the closet,' Buz said.

P.B. opened the closet. He felt uncomfortable. Nervous for some reason. Maybe he was waiting for Buz to froth at the mouth, fall about on the floor, go nuts. No danger. Not big Buz Campbell. Buz would store his grief until an appropriate time, until he had a Sten in his mitts and commies within range. P.B. would keep close to his pal for the next few weeks, though, just to make certain that Buz didn't do anything daft.

P.B. put his nose round the corner of the closet door.

Wire hangers held Buz's civilian pants and shirts, a lightweight coat. To the right, in the space, were dresses and sarongs, cheap cotton mostly, with one neat silk number which the kid had worn on very special occasions.

'The bag, wee man.'

A canvas grip and a cotton kitbag were folded in a corner by the shoes. P.B. brought out the kitbag. Beneath it was a small blue suitcase, the kind of case P.B.'s wife might have kept make-up in. P.B. tossed the kitbag to Buz who caught and opened it and pushed the crumpled nightdress inside. Buz stooped and fished out a pair of leather sandals from beneath the bed and stuffed them into the bag too. Brushing past P.B., he pulled the doors of the wardrobe wide open. A square of mirror winked in the light of the lamp.

P.B. said, 'Why don't y'leave it all 'til tomorrow, eh?'

'Do it now.'

'God, man, it's after midnight.'

'Now.'

'Right.'

Buz yanked clothing from the hangers, his own as well as the girl's, and plunged it into the bag. He bent his knees and took out the grip and lobbed it behind him into the middle of the floor. He did the same with the small blue suitcase.

'What're you goin' t' do with it all?' the Scot asked.

'Dump it.'

'Where?'

'Anywhere. Over the wall into the ocean.'

'Some of the kids in shanty-town would be glad—'

'Nope.'

P.B. didn't argue. It wasn't much, anyhow, a few cheap rags.

God, but it was a right bastard of a life when all it added up to was seventeen years of struggle, a few giggles with a Canadian old enough to be your father, and then a handful of metal blew you away out of it. Being young, being pretty, sexy and cheerful gave you no protection. If you were marked as a loser, a loser you had to be, every way.

Buz turned on his heels, still kneeling. The kitbag was bulky now, but light.

'Murder, that's what it is. Plain, friggin' murder.'

'Aye.'

'She never had a gun in her hand in her life. It wasn't like it was *her* friggin' war, was it?'

'Naw.'

'Jesus!' Buz shook his head. 'I should have quit the SAS. I shouldn't have waited. I told *her* what to do if anything happened to *me*. I mean, that's what you'd expect, right?'

'Aye, right.'

'*Me* to get the chop. It's what we're paid for. But I never dreamed . . . Seventeen years old! Christ, why does it happen?'

P.B. kept still, waiting for Buz to release it, to curse Sand Shan and all fuckin' commies for their heartlessness and treachery. But the Canadian said no more. He let his head hang for a moment then he shook it almost impatiently and, silent and dry-eyed, got to his feet. He kicked the closet door closed with his heel.

'What about these?' P.B. asked, indicating the grip and the suitcase.

'Bring 'em along.'

P.B. opened the grip and looked inside. Underclothing. Scanty little pants and a couple of brassières with tiny blue flowers worked in thread on to the cups. He felt embarrassed and sad, thinking again of his daughter, growing fast, growing safe in smoky old London town. He closed the grip and tugged the fastener. He opened the small blue suitcase – or tried to.

It was locked.

'Buz?'

The sergeant turned.

'This wee case is locked,' P.B. said.

'It ain't gonna matter.'

'What did she keep in it?'

'How do I know? I never saw inside.'

'Buz, d'you not think . . .?'

He didn't give a hoot, old Buz Campbell. The case and its contents belonged to a previous age, to a time before the raid, to a dwindling memory of happiness which he felt he would never recapture.

But when P.B. said, 'Aye, you never know,' the sergeant took the point.

He indicated his consent. P.B. kicked the spring lock with his heel, ground it until it clicked and flew open. Buz conceded to curiosity and stood by the Scot while he lifted the lid.

The case was lined with imitation velvet, with a little mirror on the inside of the lid and a couple of pockets. The soldiers had expected cosmetics and jewellery and trivial gewgaws. They were surprised to find that the case contained letters, only letters.

'What the hell!' Buz murmured.

P.B. lifted an envelope from the top. He darted a glance at Buz. 'Might be private.'

'She's dead. Nothin's private when you're dead.'

P.B. unfolded the paper. The letter was written on lined notepaper, the kind you could buy in any store, with a sharp, black lead pencil.

'Malayan?' said Buz.

'Chinese, I think,' said P.B.

Frowning, Buz got down on his knees by the case. He sifted through the letters. Some were without envelopes, some were on fine rice paper scripted in Indian ink with a flexible pen nib. Three were typed on a Malayan machine, in the language of the Peninsula. Two were in English. Two out of twenty or more.

The two in English were printed in a childish hand, large, sprawling capitals which wandered across the page. They were birthday greetings to Susu from a child, her sister, who was proud of her accomplishment in learning to write in English. The postmarks on the brown envelopes which accompanied the English letters indicated Kuala Lumpur and the date was two years ago. There was no address.

P.B. said, 'I thought she hadn't any folks?'

'She hadn't. Leastwise, none she told me about.'

'What about this wee sister, then?'

'Maybe she died before Susu came north.'

'Buz. This's her sister, her wee sister.'

'Yeah.'

'Can't you read Malayan?'

'Not enough of it.' The sergeant got to his feet. 'Bundle them back in the case. It ain't our business. The girl's dead, goddamn it!'

'She didn't tell you the truth, Buz, not the whole truth, anyhow.'

'Maybe she didn't want to worry me.'

'Worry you? How?'

'With a family. Maybe she thought . . . *Shit!*'

'Look at it, though. Dozens of bloody letters from different folk. I mean, what do they say?'

'I don't wanna know what they say. It's like pryin' into secrets that don't concern us.'

'Aye, but secrets do concern us, Buz.'

'Susu wasn't a goddamned informer, if that's what you mean.'

'Naw, naw!' said P.B., diplomatically. 'But think of it, Buz. Who's goin' to tell her wee sister and the rest of the family that Susu's dead, eh? You'll have her buried an' none of them'll know about it.'

P.B. picked up the suitcase and dumped it on the bed. Standing up to the sergeant, he jerked his thumb at the collection.

'Canny do it, Buz. Best find somebody who can interpret these bloody things, at least t'find out where her family stays.'

'Forget it. I tell you, forget it.'

'How can y' forget the ones written in Chinese? Let me show them to the Deke. He'll know what t'do for the best. Listen, the blokes in the Intelligence Section can—'

'It's private,' Buz shouted. 'Hear me, wee man? *Private.* I didn't mean what I said – about the dead.'

'Buz,' said P.B. McNair, 'the poor lassie's past carin'.'

Buz covered his face with his hand and let out breath in a ragged explosion of sound. 'Yeah, okay! We'll take them to Hauser. Hauser can read Chink.'

Mr Hauser had spent several hours at Police Headquarters being questioned about the Paradise Gardens' security. He was grilled – there was no other word for it – about his girls, what they did with the soldiers and whether he got payment from that source. It was no secret what sort of services Hauser provided and the morality, or lack of it, which lay behind the Paradise had never before been questioned.

Mr Hauser expected no favours from the police. He did not resent the fact that they treated him as if he was the perpetrator of a crime instead of one of its victims. He answered all questions truthfully, though with discretion. He was eventually released at a quarter past two o'clock in the morning. He returned by taxi-cab to his house, a sprawling apartment above the kitchens of the Gardens' main block. There were soldiers everywhere in the grounds, not in search of pleasure and relaxation now, but on duty. They aided the many uniformed policemen who were picking over the ground under the trees and, with huge, sinister torches, combed the beach for clues as to the identity of the attackers.

Mr Hauser entered by the kitchen door and found there, to his surprise, Sergeant Campbell and the Scottish corporal, both of them in civvies. Mr Hauser had been informed that the girl, Susu, was dead. He gave a bow to Sergeant Campbell and offered his hand.

Buz hesitated then took the dry, old leathery hand and shook it.

It was a token of condolence, of respect for the dead. European or Asian, the gesture was enough. Mr Hauser had no need to embellish it with flowery phrases. They were both men of the world and knew what Susu Mafan had been; but also what she had meant to each of them. Mr Hauser was no cynic. He liked the company of the little Chinese and Malayan flowers. The girls who worked for him were not so very different from his daughters. It was not difficult to understand how a lonely man like Campbell could lose his heart to one of them.

On the wooden serving-board by the still-warm stoves, there was a blue suitcase, a vanity case. Many of the girls had similar little cases, cashés where they kept their treasured belongings. Mr Hauser assumed that the one which had been brought into his kitchen had been the property of Susu Mafan. He was a man of much experience and his Germanic lineage had never quite been washed out by forty years living in the south-east of Asia.

Pragmatically he said, 'It is the girl's case, and it contains letters.'

'Yeah! How did you know?'

Mr Hauser shrugged.

'With permission?'

Buz nodded. The German lifted the lid of the case. His eyes widened a little in surprise.

'So very many letters. She had no family. Where did they come from? How did she get them? She received no mail from here, I give you my word.'

'It's family,' said P.B. 'Some of them, anyway. Can you read them, Mr Hauser?'

The German sifted through the letters, spread several out upon the board. He fished in his rumpled white dinner-jacket and took out a pair of spectacles which he perched upon his nose. He lifted one of the rice-paper leaves and held it to the light.

'Yah. I can decipher.'

'An' the others?'

Another sheet was held to the light.

'Yah. No problem for reading,' said Mr Hauser. 'But it will take time. You are wishing me to read them all?'

'Aye,' said P.B. 'You know what we're lookin' for, Mr Hauser.'

The German said, 'I thought the poor child was honest.'

It was on the tip of P.B.'s tongue to say 'We all make mistakes', but he checked himself. Buz was still in the sort of mood whereby he might snatch up the suitcase and dive off into the night with it.

P.B. said, 'She probably was – in most ways. It'll do no harm t' scan a few of those, though, just t' make certain.'

Mr Hauser pulled up a tall stool and seated himself at the board. He gave a wave of the hand. 'Please, make coffee. There should be water in the urn.'

'How long will this take?' asked Buz.

'Not long,' said Mr Hauser.

Late though it was, Deacon called Allison at the St John's. He could not explain why, but he was concerned about her. With Shan's butchers loose in the Port, anything might happen. Deacon suffered the irrational fear that, somehow, Shan might have targeted the hotel for attack. All, however, was quiet. He explained to Allison what had occurred, told her that he would not be returning that night, possibly not for several days. The woman did not question him. She understood perfectly. That done, Deacon went in search of Campbell and McNair.

'Haven't been seen, Captain,' he was informed. 'Not since this afternoon.'

'Haven't they reported in?'

The Duty Clerk shook his head. 'Tried the guard room, sir?'

'Yes,' said Deacon. 'They haven't checked through.'

The Duty Clerk, also a Scot, said, 'I have the injured list, an' they're no' on that.'

'May I see it?'

The clerk pushed the carbon across the desk.

Deacon scanned it quickly. 'What about the dead?'

'Here, sir.' The clerk gave him a second sheet. Familiar names leapt at Deacon. To all appearances it was just another piece of army bumph, typed on one of the station's old Underwoods.

'Civilians?'

'I don't have that information yet.' The clerk squinted up through the haze of cigarette smoke over the desk. 'Didn't you hear, though?'

'Hear what?' said Deacon.

'Buz's – Sergeant Campbell's – his friend, his girl . . .'

'The Chinese girl, Susu Mafan?'

'That's her; she got the chop.'

'Dead?'

'Blown apart. On the dance deck at the Paradise.'

'Was Campbell with her at the time?'

'Aye, sir. So maybe he's stayed at the hospital.'

'Damn!' said Deacon, softly. 'Damn! Damn! Damn!'

He was half-inclined to go into the Port in search of Buz and P.B. Common sense told him, however, that whatever sort of state the Canadian was in, P.B. would look out for him, make sure that he did not fly off the handle. It was possible that they were, in fact, still at the hospital, though Deacon could see no reason why they would choose to hang about if the girl was dead.

'Call the guard room, please, Corporal. When Campbell or McNair reports in, please let me know immediately. I'll be in the officers' quarters, Hut Two, probably. Will you see to it that I'm wakened at once?'

'Will do, sir.'

In spite of all that had happened, Deacon slept deeply. It was a knack he had learned many years ago. He willed himself quickly to sleep in the cot in the four-bed room in the officers' quarters. Pawson, and a young lieutenant newly arrived from the Huddersfields, were there too, snoring inside their mosquito-net shrouds.

It was close to dawn, 05.20 hours, when a guard-room private clumped into the room and shook the captain's arm.

Deacon wakened instantly.

'Is Sergeant Campbell back?'

'No, sir. CO wants you in his office right away.'

'Thank you.' Deacon hoisted his legs out of the bed.

From the adjacent cot Pawson drowsily enquired, 'What's the flap?'

'The Beezer requires my presence,' Deacon said.

'At this hour? What's amiss, old chap?'

'Lord knows!' said Deacon.

*

From whence the Number One Copper had come, Deacon had no idea. No trains reached the Port at that ungodly hour of the night. It was improbable that the great Augustus would risk a drive along the quiet country roads without a full armed escort. Not that Augustus Saunders had a lily liver. Far from it. He was a man of amazing audacity, motivated by outrageous egotism into acts of courage which few would dare emulate. As a rule he packed no weapons. As a rule he travelled with a minimum entourage. As a rule he would not hesitate to plunge into a native hut or a *kampoung* all on his own. He should have died a dozen times in the year and a half of his tenure, but fate, and an instinct for calculating the odds to the fifth decimal point, had kept the old devil alive and brought him 'a bag' of big name guerrillas from the south part of the Peninsula.

The colonel's methods of interrogation were suspect, though nobody dared question them openly. He used bribery, extortion and connivance without compunction. He had been known to lure guerrillas out of the jungle by spreading word of what was happening to their women back in the cells at Security Branch head office in Metarack. Nothing much was happening to their women, except that they were being well-fed and spooned a good deal of seductive philosophy from the maestro himself. Paternal firmness and English charm got the colonel what he wanted from wives and sweethearts. Nothing was calculated to drive a Communist wilder than a photograph of his baby son gurgling in the arms of Number One Copper and his little wife gazing adoringly at the tall Englishman. Whether the photograph was blazoned on the front page of the *Straits Times* – and many were – or came stuck into a pack of letters from the town, mattered not. Nobody, not even a jungle hoodlum, wants to lose his family to the wiles of the enemy.

Colonel Augustus Saunders was a one-man travelling circus of speciality acts. He would be one of a party of six SB thugs on an interior expedition on Tuesday, visible to the cowering commies in the trees. On Wednesday, he would be introducing reformed communists to the High Commissioner at a Garden Party in Malacca, and smiling for the photographers. That same evening he might turn up in a settlement camp in north Johore or, without pressman in attendance, be seated in a native shack in a squatter slum in the Kota Tinggi, cooking up a trade with a highly nervous turncoat.

Colonel Saunders had his own very private funds and his own methods. By most of the brass with whom he had dealings, he was regarded as a big fat show-off. But he did get results. No question of that. He netted commies the way a Yarmouth fisherman nets sprats. He was not, however, particularly cooperative with military staff when it came to exchanging information, though he expected them to jump when he demanded it.

Showered, shaved and in a fresh uniform, the Beezer was dispensing coffee from a red metal pot.

'Ah, Deacon. I believe you know Colonel Saunders.'

The colonel turned. He was exceedingly tall and dipped his head, thus giving the impression that he was peering disapprovingly at the captain, which might very well have been the case.

Deacon said, 'I do, indeed.'

'Deacon. Yes, I remember you,' said Saunders.

The colonel and the captain shook hands while the Beezer watched curiously. The CO was sensitive to delicate situations and he was aware that one might be developing before his eyes. In the Beezer's view, Deacon would be panting to get into the jungle and after Sand Shan. Now that Saunders was here, however, the Security and Police branches would want things done their way. A spirit of competition was commendable at times but in soldiering in Malaya it had its drawbacks.

Deacon said, 'How is your daughter, Colonel?'

'Gone back to England. Climate didn't suit her.'

'I see,' said Deacon.

Saunders drank coffee. He did it with a swift tilt of the elbow and drained the cup in one swallow, as if to be rid of it. He rattled the cup into the saucer and slid it on to the tray.

'A touch more, Colonel Saunders?' said the Beezer, hospitably.

Saunders ignored him. He put his hands behind his back and studied Deacon. It was not quite light yet. The lamps burned under green metal shades, making an island around the major's desk. A large black fly buzzed among the moths and in the cool, clear, pre-dawn air outside, birds shrilled.

'Bad show,' Saunders said. 'Catchin' Kwai Yan Chung then losin' him again. Bad show.'

'Kwai Yan Chung wasn't exactly lost,' said Deacon, evenly. 'He was assassinated.'

'Sloppy. Very sloppy,' said Saunders.

'Police department, not SAS responsibility,' said Major Beasley.

'I'm not denying it,' said Saunders.

'After all,' said the Beezer, 'it is one bandit less.'

'Damn it, Major, I could have wrung information out of Kwai Yan Chung. Unbelievable amounts of information. I could have persuaded him to point the finger at Sand Shan.'

'Really?' said Deacon. 'Kwai Yan Chung might have been a tougher nut than you're used to, Colonel.'

Saunders gave a bark of laughter. 'I *crush* tough nuts, Captain Deacon. Crush 'em like beetles.'

The Beezer cleared his throat. 'I'm afraid we can't offer you much by way of "raw material". The killer squad did its work too blessed well.'

Hands still behind his back, Saunders strolled up and down the length of the office. 'There will be somethin' for us to pick up. Always is. Some coolie'll come out of the bush beggin' to play the Judas.'

'Perhaps my lads will pick up something useful.'

Saunders glanced quickly at the major. 'Your lads?'

'As soon as I have the say-so from my superiors,' said Beasley, 'we'll be pushing out into the countryside again. In force.'

'No, you won't.'

'Pardon?' said the Beezer.

'Maintain routine patrols, o'course,' said Saunders. 'But I don't want your lot crashing into the bush like a herd of buffalo. Sorry I've got to be blunt, Major.'

'If I'm ordered—'

'You won't be ordered.'

'Colonel Saunders,' said the Beezer, 'may I remind you that you don't hold sway over the SAS.'

'But I do have cooperation.'

'Shan must be found and punished.'

'I've been hearin' that since I set foot in Malaya,' said Saunders. 'If not Shan, some other jackanapes. These are peasants, Major. They haven't got an ounce of sense. Sly, yes. But clever – no, that they aren't.'

Deacon wondered how Saunders could have built himself a success record on such a naïve premise. Sand Shan might be a peasant by birth but he had been educated and given experience in the Japanese war, and had a mind as sharp as a *kris*. Did Saunders not see just how brilliantly executed the raid on Port Kernan had been? For a start, Shan had struck without delay. He had assembled, briefed and put in three trained killer squads in a matter of days. Four days since the first RAF bomb fell on the Totan, in fact. Shan had wasted not a single moment in making his decision and in implementing it. Did Saunders suppose that this was luck, or the casual labour of a 'little bandit'?

Deacon said, 'Perhaps the colonel has a lead?'

The colonel's expression changed instantly to one of suspicion. 'Lead? Who said anything about a lead?'

'I imagined,' said Deacon, 'that you didn't want us to queer the pitch . . .'

'I don't.'

'. . . because you have a strong lead as to where we might lay hands on Shan?'

'This is your territory, Deacon, not mine,' said Saunders. 'Where on earth would I get a lead on Shan?'

'In the city,' said Deacon. 'Through his Fat Cat, his officer of supply.'

'Which city?' said Saunders.

Deacon shrugged lightly. 'Singapore, Malacca, K.L. – I have absolutely no idea.'

Saunders smiled. 'Neither do I.'

'What do you propose to do, Colonel?' put in the Beezer.

'Nose around. I've got a fine hooter.' Saunders tapped his nose. 'Picks up scents others miss.'

'How can we assist?' asked the Beezer, stiffly.

'Bring me the files,' said Saunders.

'Files on what?'

'Ops.'

'All of them?'

'Every single one.'

'Will that be all?' said the Beezer.

'I'll need the use of an office. One with a lock on the door.'

'Certainly, Colonel,' said the Beezer.

'I'll want to talk to your men, too. Those of 'em that were on the scene tonight.'

'Scene?' said the Beezer.

'At this brothel or whatever it is; the Paradise Gardens.'

'My chaps—'

'I won't be any trouble, Major Beasley. Be quiet as a mouse,' said Saunders.

'My chaps—'

Saunders turned. 'Let's start right off, will we? Let's start the ball rollin' at once.'

Deacon said, 'I assume that you believe Sand Shan had inside information on the disposition of British forces?'

Saunders' expression screwed into suspicion again. He darted a malicious glance at the captain. 'Nothin' of the kind.'

Deacon said, 'I would have thought it obvious that Sand Shan received his intelligence on certain matters from within Port Kernan itself, though not necessarily directly from an SAS man or other member of the British forces.'

'Obvious?'

'It wasn't guesswork, Colonel,' said Deacon. 'Shan *knew* when Kwai Yan Chung would be brought into the Port. He *knew* that the prisoners were housed in the jail and that the wounded were being kept in the St Andrew's hospital.'

'There are commie sympathisers everywhere, Captain,' said Saunders. 'But you're spot-on in your guess. Yes, I *have* reason to believe that Shan got his up-to-the-minute information through this post.'

'Not, perhaps, from one of the policemen at the gaol-house?'

'One of your own men, Captain Deacon. One in particular.'

'Oh, really? Which one?'

'A sergeant by the name of Campbell.'

Big man on the mountain

The bus which left Port Kernan every morning at seven o'clock took between five and seven hours, depending on the state of roads and weather, to wend its way to Kuala Lumpur. That particular morning, however, there were few passengers and the sun shone. Once road-blocks and inspection points were left behind, the Leyland single-decker came into its own and the bright-eyed Malay at the wheel put his foot down and fairly licked up the miles.

There were three women with baskets, a couple of Indians and two white men on board. A family of four, a mother and three young children, were picked up at Genting Jugra where the bus was again searched by a road patrol, this time from the Fusiliers.

Buz and P.B. extended their cards of identity.

The corporal in charge of the detail studied them.

'Comin' down frum the Port, then, S'ar'nt?'

'That's right, son.'

'Eh, got yer ticket, like?'

'Not on leave. No pass.'

'How come, then? I thought all your lot'd be on Alert.'

'We are,' said P. B. McNair, glibly. 'But we've got a wee bit of business, official-unofficial, t'do in K.L., see.'

'Rotten do for your lot last night,' said the corporal, returning the cards. 'Was it as bad's we've heard, like?'

'Yeah, pretty goddamned bad. That's why we're on this jalopy, 'stead of truckin' it,' Buz lied. 'Anyhow, Captain Deacon didn't want us crashin' into Kuala wavin' the flag. Right?'

'Captain Deacon? Is he your CO?' said the corporal, impressed.

'Squad commander,' said P.B., with a modest smile.

'Heard about 'im, like.'

'Anyway,' said P.B., 'we got a wee bit business t' do in Kuala Lumpur – concernin' last night's stramash.'

'Yer? Under the hat, like?'

'Under the hat,' said Buz.

Minutes later, the corporal waved the bus away and the vehicle rolled along the clearway to the end of the pass and into the jungle once more.

P.B. said, 'I never thought it'd be so bloody easy to go over the hill.'

Grimly, Buz said, 'We ain't goin' over the hill. We got passes 'til Sunday; three days yet.'

'Aye, but . . .'

'You didn't have to come.'

'We should've told somebody.'

'If we'd told anybody – even the Deke – we'd've been hauled back.'

'Aye, that's what worries me.'

'It's my business. You can frig off any time, wee man,' said Buz.

'Ach, no. How were you t'know Susu was an informer?'

'We don't know that, not yet.'

P.B. sighed.

He was wearing a pair of expensive flannels and a dark brown hound's-tooth blazer which Mr Hauser had kindly produced from his wardrobe. P.B. did not feel entirely comfortable in them. He did not feel at all comfortable in the situation to which his loyalty to the big Canadian sergeant had put him. But if he didn't accompany Buz, there's no saying what would happen, what sort of fix the daft big bugger would get himself into. He'd had a lot to put up with, right enough. Susu being killed was bad enough, Christ knows, but finding out she had lied to him was salt in the wound. Orphan? Some bloody orphan! The kid had more living relatives than the Duke of bloody Windsor. And all of them wrapped up in shady deals with the CT. What Buz had told her she had reported back to the 'family' around Kuala Lumpur and they had traded it, presumably for hard cash, to somebody called Kekao.

It was with considerable embarrassment that Mr Hauser had

translated the salient parts of the letters. He read in a low voice while Buz slouched over the chopping-board with one hand over his eyes. A right dirty, shameful business. The sweet little kid had been pumping Buz for months, squeezing him like an orange for juicy droplets of privileged information. She must have been good at it, not too obvious, or Buz – even in a love-struck state – would have twigged. Maybe it was as well the CTs had done her in. Buz would have killed her with his own bare hands if the truth had come to light in any other way. It was part of the climate of South-East Asia, a complication of the festering disease of communism.

P.B. and Mr Hauser had tried to persuade Buz to take the letters to Beasley, dump responsibility into the major's basket. But Buz was filled with rage and only action could keep him from going right over the edge. The sergeant made up his mind at once.

'We'll go see this family.'

'But, Buz, how can we get—'

'You don't have to.'

'What'll we do when we get there?'

'Grab an' hold.'

There was an address on many of the letters. The majority came from a brother by the name of Tony. The English name meant nothing, for the letters were written in Malayan or in a bastard form of Chinese which even Mr Hauser had trouble translating.

Tony Mafan was not guarded in his writing; the mystery was why Susu had kept the letters. In a town in a country where the police might raid at any time, it was a silly and dangerous thing to do. The letters originated in a suburb of Kuala Lumpur, a Chinese shanty-town out of which street vendors came to set up stalls for the night markets in K.L.'s Petaling Street. Mr Hauser knew it, a recent settlement with hosts of incomers living in box-like prefabricated shacks which rack-rent landlords had slung up purportedly to house factory labour.

Kuala Lumpur had long been the British capital on the Peninsula, a tin-mining centre slung between the muddy rivers of Klang and Gombek. The town was pierced by ornate mosques. Even the railway station was bizarrely Moorish. Buz and P.B. had spent very little time in Kuala Lumpur but Mr Hauser had furnished them with a pocket guide and had thoughtfully marked upon it the places mentioned in Tony Mafan's letter.

P.B. had no notion of what they, a couple of rough-neck soldiers, could hope to wring out of Tony Mafan, who was obviously only one member of a full-blown Red cell. But once they were on the bus and headed down the coast, the Scot relaxed enough to catch some sleep, wakening only when Buz shook him by the arm.

'Let's go.'

'Are we there, then?'

'No sense goin' into town,' said Buz. 'We get out here, we can hike it.'

'What about eatin'?'

'We can eat later.'

P.B. nodded; he had expected something like this.

They left the bus six miles out of town. They found themselves on the long spike of the north road which smeared into the Jl Tuanku Abdul Rahman. The 'village' where Mafan lived was just outside the gazetted limits of the town itself. Urbanisation had been rapid and largely uncontrolled. Even here there was much noise and traffic, dust and hot smells. The SAS men, used to the great green peace of jungle and swamp, and sedate Port Kernan, found it at first confusing.

There was no macadam surface to the side streets which patterned the clapboard bungalows. Ragged palms clung to the beaten earth of side lots. It was a place like no other P.B. had ever seen, an unwholesome mixture of city and country. Broken pavements skittered into sand and stunted bushes around the 'scheme's' regular box-shaped dwellings. Porches had been built on by industrious tenants, sagging decks of timber and corrugated iron. Canvas tents by the paths gave shade to vegetables cultivated in gardens no larger than hearthrugs. There were telephone poles, but no street lights.

On one stretch the water main ran above ground, perched on a wooden trestle. Pigs fattened along the scrub edge behind the box-dwellings. There were women, mostly Chinese, in many of the gardens and porches.

Buz and the Scots corporal stood out like sore thumbs as they walked quickly along the back-roads of the quarter. The layout was chequerboard. Mr Hauser had pencilled a circle around the place where the Mafan house might be found. Women and some elderly men came out to see the sight of off-duty soldiers in the Reka Kekang. The only soldiers that the denizens of the quarter ever saw were the armed and uniformed kind who came with coppers in blaring jeeps to storm houses of communist suspects, to lift young men for questioning.

'Look at that,' said P.B.

The bus-stop was painted red and yellow in barber's-pole stripes and stood ten feet high, growing from a massive lump of concrete set upon the edge of the road. It was crowned with a sign: *Factory Bus. Wait Here*. The instruction was repeated in Chinese script.

'Maybe Mafan's no' here at all,' said P.B.

'At the factory, you mean?'

'Aye.'

'Then we'll wait.'

'Listen, Buz. Direct action's one thing, but stupidity's another. I'm no' goin' to be anywhere near here after dark. You know what they're like. Mafan'll have word about us as soon as he leaves the factory gate. It'll be all over K.L. in fifteen bloody minutes.'

'We don't get him today. We get him tomorrow.'

'Aye, maybe.'

'At the factory.'

'I still think we should've reported—'

'Stop bleatin', wee man.'

'There's the house,' said P. B. McNair.

Colonel Saunders, in shirtsleeves, looked up from the bundle of papers on the desk. He had been given one of the Education

Block lecture rooms, a safe distance from the Admin Block and the Beezer's office. Clerks had equipped it for his comfort with borrowed chairs and other necessary furniture. A civilian 'boy' had been allotted as batman and runner and the poor Malay had spent a busy morning keeping the copper supplied with tea.

'Have you found him?' Saunders asked.

Deacon said, 'Not yet, Colonel.'

'I got the impression that Campbell was a veteran.'

'He is, sir.'

'Don't he know better than to slope off when the squadrons are in a state of full alert?'

'Why is Campbell so important to you, Colonel Saunders?'

'Friend of yours?'

'Of long standing,' said Deacon.

'Wouldn't be you who brought him in again, would it?'

'Yes.'

'Can't be bothered with this regimental nonsense you chaps in the SAS are so addicted to; the three musketeers' attitude.'

'We aren't the only outfit in the army who—' Deacon bit off the comment. He was not obliged to justify himself or the regiment to this man.

'Are the police lookin' out for Campbell?' asked Saunders.

'Yes.'

Saunders closed the file on top of the bundle and pushed it to one side. He extracted another document from a wire tray; Buz Campbell's service record, the version 'doctored' by Tim Dalinart. Saunders studied it.

'A ladies' man, Campbell?' he murmured.

'Not particularly,' said Deacon.

'But he has a whore in town, doesn't he? A permanent arrangement with one of the girls? Lives with her when he's not on duty?'

'I don't believe that sort of information is on record.'

'Of course it isn't.'

Deacon began to pick up a sense of what Saunders was driving at, a cold, unpleasant feeling in the gut.

Deacon said, 'I have other duties, Colonel, if you're . . .'

Saunders steepled his fingers in front of his chest, as if piously seeking Divine guidance on the matter of whether or not to trust this aristocratic officer with the implacable blue eyes and a permanent expression of disdain.

'I didn't fetch in the information about Campbell from his records. I didn't even have to sniff about the mess. Came on it from the other end.'

Deacon, who had remained standing, now drew out a chair and, without invitation, seated himself. He fixed the copper intently. 'Are you sure you want to tell me this, Colonel?'

'You're a brave chap, Captain. You're all brave chaps. Even this Sergeant Campbell. But you have no cunnin'. Batterin' rams, that's what you lot are. Batterin' rams. Heads down and charge.'

Again Deacon restrained himself from protest.

Saunders went on, 'Campbell's name cropped up in the course of a little interrogation down in Singapore. Long way from here, isn't it? Now, you've got my word I didn't have the coolie strung up by his pillocks or anythin' nasty. He came in voluntarily and wanted a deal from us.'

'How informed, how important was this prisoner?'

'He claimed to be a courier.'

'For Shan's outfit?'

'Yes, and others too.'

'Did you substantiate his claim?'

'It wasn't too difficult,' said Saunders. 'In any case, it came to light that there *is* an organisation which victuals Shan's units, and pays out money. His various units are all paid. Forty dollars a month for an infantry soldier.'

'Who gives them American arms?'

'A Chinese Fat Cat,' said Saunders.

'Do you know this person's name?'

'My prisoner couldn't supply it.'

'Couldn't, or wouldn't?'

'Couldn't. When he blabbed the whole story, I believed him. It's a very tidy little spy cell. Very Russian, if you know what I mean. All the parts fit together neatly, but nobody is supposed to know anybody else.'

Deacon said, 'What's the cell's connection with the official Malayan Communist Party, and is it associated with the Min Yuen?'

'No connection with either I've been able to discover.'

'That explains a great deal, Colonel.'

'Does it, Jeff?'

The sudden switch to informality did not put Deacon off his guard.

'It explains why Sand Shan has been able to operate effectively over so wide a field and for so long. He's simply better at it than his brethren who work "officially".'

'A lone wolf,' said Saunders.

'Hardly a lone wolf,' said Deacon. 'Wolves don't kill their own kind, do they?'

Saunders said, 'Sand Shan has – usually – been able to keep one hop ahead of you and the rest of the Security Forces because of his informants. He pays out a lot of dollars to spies at ground level.'

'Does Shan do the paying,' asked Deacon, 'or is it the Fat Cat who attends to that sort of thing?'

'Probably the Fat Cat,' said Saunders.

'Where does Buz Campbell fit into the picture?'

'The little Chinkie trollop named Mafan was the "ear" in Port Kernan. Regarded as a jolly jape by the coolies in K.L. and Singapore that she'd got a string on such a big hero.'

'Was Buz Campbell's name mentioned?'

'Referred to as "the sergeant". Fair enough?'

'Buz wouldn't sell information.'

'Of course he wouldn't. Not suggestin' he did. But he leaked it, nonetheless. Pillow talk. This girl was in the right place for information-gatherin'. She had a front-line patrol NCO in the sheets with her. She could get what she needed without half tryin'.'

'You are aware that the girl was killed last night?'

Saunders nodded.

Deacon said, 'If you knew all this, why didn't you put a stop to it? Confine Buz Campbell to barracks? At least give some indication?'

'I only discovered the truth last week. Campbell was on patrol. He couldn't do any harm up-country, could he? I was due here and thought I'd kill more than one bird with my stone.'

'All right, Colonel Saunders,' said Deacon. 'But with the girl dead, surely the trail ends? Buz won't know who her connections were.'

'I know who her direct connection is,' said Saunders. 'A family in the factory district outside of Kuala. Particularly a brother. Tony, that's what he calls himself.'

'Haven't you picked him up for questioning?'

'Not interested in small fry.'

'Only in my sergeant?'

Saunders said, 'I want the Fat Cat, the big man on the mountain. Stop the supply of dollars, arms and food and we'll whittle away Shan's battalions in no time at all. Most of the guerrillas aren't in it for anythin' other than profit. It's a job they can do without much effort, and it pays well.'

Deacon said, 'And you want Buz Campbell to help?'

'We might be able to work together.'

'Syrup, Colonel?' said Deacon.

Saunders had the decency to smile. 'To tell the truth, my friend, you've had your shot at Sand Shan. It's my turn at the wicket now.'

'Shan will be buried deep again.'

'Not at all, not at all. That's always been the army failing, the assumption that Shan spends his days under a palm leaf in the middle of an impenetrable swamp. Nothin' of the kind. Shan stays a jump ahead of you because he's never where you think he should be. He wasn't at the camp in the Totan, for instance.'

'That's true,' said Deacon.

'Perhaps he had an inkling that the camp was goin' to be raided.'

'Via the girl, do you mean?'

'God knows!' said Saunders.

'Surely, Colonel, not even Sand Shan would let an established training camp fall to enemy attack without trying to prevent it?'

'Your reason for thinkin' that might not be Shan's reason.'

'Shan's not stupid.'

Saunders lifted his shoulders and spread his hands. 'Why wasn't he there?'

'Luck,' said Deacon.

'Sounds a bit lame, don't it?'

'But if Campbell did leak it to the girl and she in turn fed it through the pipeline, and word of our intention reached Shan—'

'And Shan just happened to be two or three hundred miles away,' Saunders interrupted, 'he isn't goin' to rush back into that swamp country.'

'He could have sent a radio message.'

'Your Canadian sergeant couldn't have told the girl when the strike would occur,' said Saunders. 'Though Shan must have known when the supply column was due to reach his camp.'

'I'm confused, Colonel. What are you driving at?'

'Confusion, that's the word,' said Saunders. 'There are seventy thousand policemen, includin' five thousand specialists, in this country, plus all you chaps with Brens and airplanes and the like, and none of you has been able to throw a net across this bandit or his bosses. But *he* manages to raid your town, storm the jail and the hospital, and walk right into the recreation area . . .'

'Please, Colonel Saunders, come to the point.'

'I can use Campbell to bring Shan to a particular place at a particular time. And we'll be there before him. I want the sergeant to cooperate, Jeff. You're his chum, his comrade and his superior officer. Now, where is he?'

Deacon hesitated. He could see – dimly – what the devious

copper had in mind. But with the girl dead and the connection with the communist cell broken, he could not fathom how the colonel intended to use Buz Campbell.

'I suspect,' Deacon said, cautiously, 'that Buz has beaten us to it.'

'What the hell do you mean?'

'I believe that my sergeant may have gone hunting.'

With a face as black as a thunder cloud, Saunders shot to his feet and shouted, 'He damned well better not have. The last thing I want's a rogue runnin' loose.'

'I'm afraid that's what we might have.'

'If he damages my contacts,' Saunders raged, 'I'll have him broken, tossed out of the—'

'Threats won't deter Buz Campbell.'

'Come again?'

'The sergeant has nothing left to lose.'

Tony Mafan had been born under the star of China. He had been spawned by a pre-Maoist rebel who had taken a fourteen-year-old village girl against her will then gone his way again, leaving her pregnant, with a chocolate bar in her scraggy little hand by way of compensation. The girl hadn't a clue what the rebel's name was but she invented one for him and passed it on to her first-born, calling him Lee Lu Chang, which handle lasted through five years of war until the boy was old enough and wise enough to change it to Tony Mafan.

With his brown hair brush-cut, in a pair of denim shorts, a gaudy Bermuda shirt, tennis sox and Keds, Tony might have passed as a poor boy from UCLA, except for the thick, gold-plated Movado Calendolux watch on his wrist, three fancy rings, one of gold, and the mass of gadgets which crammed the square kitchen of the prefabricated house.

A Columbia wireless set, oak with red glass inserts, trailed its cable through a tangle of other wires. A Westinghouse toaster and a Peek-a-Brew coffee percolator were both in operation and the G.E. water filter which fitted over the sink tap gave off a strident hum so that Tony had to stoop and twiddle with the tuner of the Columbia to try to catch snippets of news about the big raid in Port Kernan.

The strike had come too late in the evening to make the morning editions of the newspapers. Tony was dependent, so far, on the garbled accounts that Foster Maclean, reporter for the BBC Malayan News Service, was putting together by the hour. Tony chuckled as the figures were announced, and gave little theatrical yelps of glee, saying to himself, in a phoney American accent, 'Yeah! Yeah! Hot shit, yeah!'

The internment camp where Tony and his Ma and four siblings, including Susu, had wound up had been in American possession for eighteen months, and Tony had been smack in the middle of his most formative years. It was there he had learned respect – reverence, you might say – for the American lifestyle with its accent on comfort and material possessions, and had switched over from the traditional religions of a displaced rebel to emulation through acquisition. By the age of thirteen, Tony had become the head of the house of Mafan, bread-winner number one, arrogantly bossing around his Ma and his sisters and selling anything – yeah, anything – he could find a market for, which included his Ma's time and his sisters' virginity and, pretty soon after, information.

Tony worked for a guy called Kekao who ran a little printing shop in Kuala Lumpur's Treacher Street, a neat brick office where local advertising handbills and 'educational' material of an innocent kind were inked up on an old-fashioned press. Not that Tony ever got his fingers dirty. He wasn't one of Kekao's printers, though he got paid through Kekao's books and picked up his bonuses – the Movado, the Columbia, the Westinghouse, etc. – from the front counter. Anyhow, Kekao wasn't really important.

Behind Kekao there was the big man. Tony figured he could finger the big man any time he wanted to exert himself, though he'd never do it, of course, since he didn't want to wind up floating in the mud of the Gombek, or disappearing without trace into the Selangor, which is what happened to hirelings who got a mite too sharp. He earned his bucks and had a good life. He would hoist himself further up the ladder in course of time, long before the Brits flushed the Reds out of Malaya.

But time for Tony Mafan was running out quicker than he imagined.

Tony settled the station for the two o'clock news broadcast, pulled himself a cup of java from the perker, lit a Marlboro with his Zippo lighter and leaned against the Dutch dresser.

The screen door at the back of the kitchen darkened with the outline of the boy Tony kept on the payroll. In Malay dialect, sprinkled with Chinese and American phrases, the boy, an eleven-year-old, told Tony Mafan that two strangers, whites, were coming down the street.

Tony hit the centre switch on the panel which put off all the electrical current in the house. He slid to the window. He lifted the sun-blind slats with his thumbnail and peered down the short avenue by the house side, towards the gate.

One white guy, a small guy, was coming up the path.

Tony's gun was a snub-nosed Colt .38 Police Special which he stored out of harm's way in one of the blackened pots which his Ma had brought with her out of the camps. Ducking, Tony snapped open the closet under the sink, hauled out the pot and dug the gun from inside. He scooped up a handful of shells and loaded the Colt expertly, six shots, spun the chambers and, with the weapon in his hand, stepped softly to the door which connected the kitchen to the house's front hall. From there he could see the path and the porch. There were two fly-screen doors and a wooden frame door between him and the stranger. The frame door was hooked open to keep the fore-part of the house cool.

Tony tucked the gun under the flap of his shirt at waist level and held it. He didn't care if the guy guessed that he was carrying artillery.

Ma was out of the way, his sister Lily too. They were both on the packing line up in the shoe factory, earning good bread for an eight-hour shift. Ma said the work was not difficult and she enjoyed the company of the other girls, most of whom, though not all, were about Lily's age. Mainly, the job got Ma and the kid out of the house.

The thing Tony had always feared seemed to be happening. The guys weren't soldiers. They were coppers. They were a pair picked from the new bunch, the detectives that Saunders had trained specially to work under cover. But they were too obvious. Anybody born east of the Tropic could spot them a mile off. Saunders' bloodhounds.

There was only one of them in sight, on the path, not doing anything very much, just hanging around with his hands in his pockets and a cigarette stuck to his bottom lip. He wasn't looking right or left, was staring at the screen door of the porch.

The boy was still in the kitchen. Tony glanced behind him.

The boy was not in the kitchen.

The rear door stood wide open. It was as if a tiger had prowled through the door and carried the kid away, silently, in its mouth.

Tony brought out the gun.

The kitchen was empty.

Tony whirled.

The path was deserted.

A cigarette lay on the dirt, wisping smoke.

Tony Mafan sucked in a shuddering breath. The Colt Special gave him no particular comfort now. This wasn't anything he had bargained for. He had always figured that if the connections blew and the coppers came for him they would come straight and he would be able to get out before they could jig him. He had been interrogated – well, questioned – a couple of times before. But the detectives, if they were detectives, which he was beginning to doubt, had short-circuited his plans.

Not quite all his plans, though. He still had an emergency exit – through the tiny window in the bedroom which Lily and Ma shared. The window came all the way out and he could get up on to the roof from there. He had practised the manoeuvre. Once he was on the roof he could slither along it like a lizard and use a rope he had slung from a dusty Chiku tree to get down into the neighbour's plot where there was a clutter of outbuildings and a gate in the back fence into the lane.

Tony Mafan took a last look at the kitchen. The door swung gently on its hinges. The radio played dance music. Out front, there was no sign of the white guy.

Tony decided to play it safe.

He crept into the hall and along it, left into the narrow corridor and off it into the darkened bedroom.

The room smelled of women. It was neat and spartan and the two cots were made up with silk overcovers. Ma had even had time to put a posy of nest fern and two Scorpion orchids in the glass before the Virgin, though Lily's pyjamas squirmed on the floor and she had left her bottle of Eau de Cologne open again.

Tony stepped on to Lily's cot. Two plaited ropes protruded from the frame of the window. The window in this room had been added to the house to meet some fire regulation. It provided no proper ventilation. Tony yanked out the frame and set the window down upon the cot. He muscled himself up and twisted his head, chest and shoulders through the aperture. There was an eave of sorts and an aluminium rain drain. He got his fingers over it, pulled himself smoothly out. The Colt Special was in his belt. Both hands clamped to the edge of the metal drain, his legs still within the bedroom, Tony Mafan braced himself for the pull that would take him quietly on to the roof.

The boot came down on his fingertips. The heel stamped once, twice. Tony screamed as bones broke. He tried to hang on. Looming above him, perched on the edge of the ramp of the roof, he saw a huge, brutal white man. At precisely that moment, somebody in the bedroom caught his legs. The hands were like vices around his ankles.

The man on the roof had swarthy features which betrayed neither malice nor anger, not even glee, as he methodically hammered his heel on Tony's fingers once more. Blood spurted from the fingernails. The broken ends of the bones of the knuckle joints bored into the nerves.

Screaming, Tony let go.

He fell backwards, belly out. Bow-like pressure pinned him by the ankles. The window frame hacked into the backs of his thighs. His skull cracked against the board side of the house and he hung upside down, dazed and whimpering.

The big man jumped down heavily from the edge of the roof and stood beside him. Tony could hardly see. Agony in his hands came in waves, thundering through his concussion. His head was on a level with the stranger's crotch.

The big man tugged the Colt from Tony's belt.

'Hey, kid. Know who I am?'

Tony went on whimpering.

The man bent from the waist, face close to Tony's. He put his right hand across Tony's nose and mouth and smothered the noises.

'Hey, kid. I asked you a goddamned question, right?'

Tony's eyes bugged. Blood filled his head. It felt like a ripe mango about to burst in the sun. He made gargling sounds.

The big man smiled bleakly. 'I was nearly your goddamned brother-in-law. Know that? Yeah, I was nearly family.' The fist unclamped a little from Tony's mouth. 'Got me now?'

'C . . . C . . . Cam . . .'

'Yeah. Campbell.'

'*Plise . . . plise . . .*'

'Keep it shut, okay?'

Raw fear closed Tony's mouth. He squeezed his eyes to try to regain his senses.

Campbell said, 'You got him, P.B.?'

'Aye,' growled a voice from within the house. 'I got him.'

Campbell lowered himself comfortably to the ground, back against the wall.

Tony rolled his eyes. He watched the sergeant in fascination. Blood dripped from his swollen fingers on to the dry earth, making faint pat-pat-patting sounds.

Campbell extracted a bent Marlboro from the packet which had slipped from Tony's pocket. He lit it with Tony's Zippo. He inhaled smoke, coughed and laid the Marlboro packet on the ground. The Zippo he kept in his hand.

Squatting, shoulders against the wood, Campbell said, 'Susu got her head blown off. Got in the way of a frag grenade.'

Tony uttered an almost inaudible moan.

'Nice kid, your sister. Great little lay,' said Campbell. 'She wasn't the same with her head layin' loose, though. Don't suppose you guys figured Mr Sand Shan would be so careless. Well, kid, he was. Real careless.'

Pat-pat-pat went the little droplets of contused blood into the thirsty soil. Campbell flicked the Zippo. The flame bloomed large and yellow, like silk.

Campbell said, 'You sold your sister up the fuckin' river, Tony, ain't that right? What'd you get for it? Huh? This Zippo?'

'Buz.'

'Yeah, wee man?'

'Shove it along, eh?'

'Sure, sure.'

Tony was beginning to feel nauseated. He had grasped the import of what Campbell had told him. Susu was dead. He was in no position to enjoy the luxury of grief. It had all been laid out for him, the reason why Campbell was here. The stupid little bitch must have kept his letters. He should never have written to her, not even via Mr Tang who kept the sugar stall in Port Kernan's Harbour Street and was a trustworthy servant of the communist cause. Mr Tang should never have given Susu the letters in the first place. The letters were no good to her. Susu had never learned to read properly. The only ones she could make out at all were from her cousin, and he was only a child.

Tony mumbled.

'How's that again?' said Campbell.

'I . . . I did not know she . . .'

'Sure,' Campbell said. 'A mistake, an accident. Right?'

'Plise, you let—'

Campbell flicked the Zippo petrol lighter once more.

He smiled at the soft, bright flame.

'Hey, see these gizmos, know what we use them for? Use them to toast marshmallows. Perfect for toastin' marshmallows. Nice slow heat. Hold the marshmallow on a twig, turn it over in the flame. Watch the marshmallow melt.'

Tony Mafan could only dimly recall what a marshmallow looked like. He had never eaten one in his life. But the picture was vivid enough. He began to moan in his throat again and might have screamed in terror if at that moment Campbell had not got to his feet.

Rolling his eyeballs, Tony watched as the sergeant snapped the Zippo shut, stretched his arm and deftly dropped the lighter through the open window.

'You got it, P.B.?'

'Aye.'

'You wanna toast somethin'?'

'I havenae any marshmallows, Buz.'

'Look around. See if you can find anythin' else to toast.'

Campbell came down to Mafan's level once more. Blobs of sweat dripped with the blood on to the ground. Buz put the snout of the Colt against Tony's taut throat. Within the bedroom, seemingly remote, Tony felt fingers fumble at his denim shorts.

'No. You cannot. No. Plise.'

'Son, son. I can do anythin' I fuckin' like, right now,' said the sergeant. 'I'm right in the goddamned mood, too. You ready, P.B.?'

'Aye.'

Tony Mafan felt a waft of heat against his skin. The numbness of concussion had gone and his nerves shrilled at the prospect of pain. He could not stand pain. He wasn't that sort of tough-guy.

'*Ma. Ma. Ma,*' he bellowed.

'Hold it, P.B.,' Campbell said.

'I did not know what they would do, no, no,' Tony Mafan jabbered. 'I did not know it would be with you and Susu when they threw the bombs. It was supposed to be only prisoners. I told them it would be easy to get prisoners when they—'

'Told who?'

'Kekao. I tell Kekao what Susu tells me.'

'An' who tells Susu?'

'You do, you do, you do.'

Buz Campbell sighed.

He removed the gun, slipped his hand under Tony Mafan's neck and eased the weight that gravity exerted upon the young man's spine. He cocked the head towards him so that Mafan and he were face to face and the kid had nowhere else to focus his eyes.

'Okay,' Campbell said. 'Let's you'n' me have a little talk.'

'I tell you everything.'

'Goddamned right you will,' the sergeant said.

Even the great Augustus Saunders had need of sleep from time to time. After lunch, he quit the SAS camp and was chauffeured back to the Lawrence Hotel, a small but splendid residence which overlooked Port Kernan's Royal Park Gardens. It was the sort of way-station which catered for high-ranking diplomats, top government officials and senior executives of international rubber companies, but Saunders was not the sort to stint himself on an expense account. He carried no papers and retired at once to his room on the third floor. He switched on the fan, drew the curtains, took off his shoes and jacket and settled himself on the bed with the telephone balanced on his chest. He made a series of calls, including a couple to Singapore, then composed his angular body and, lying on his back with his arms folded over his chest, fell asleep.

It was twenty minutes past four o'clock when the telephone rang. Saunders opened his eyes and instantly swept the receiver into his fist.

'Yes.'

'It's Captain Deacon.'

'Yes.'

'I'm at the desk downstairs, Colonel. I must see you at once.'

'Come up. Oh, and while you're at it, ask the boy to bring me a *stengah*.'

Saunders rose and went directly to the bathroom and peeled off his shirt. He sluiced water over his chest and head then took down his shaving kit from the shelf where his boy had placed it earlier that day. He worked up a lather in the china mug. He was vigorously stropping his cut-throat on a worn leather strap when the SAS captain arrived, together with the Malay and the whisky-soda.

'Bring it in, Jeffrey.'

Deacon carried the glass into the bathroom.

Foaming brush in one hand, the razor in the other, Saunders squinted at Deacon in the mirror.

'Trouble?'

'I'm not sure,' Deacon answered. 'I just received a telephone call from Sergeant Campbell.'

'Did you now? Where is he?'

'In K.L.,' said Deacon. 'He wants assistance.'

'What sort of assistance?' Brush and blade remained poised. 'And why did he call you?'

'He called me because he thinks he's into something important,' said Deacon. 'In addition, he's extremely upset about what's happened.'

'Wants to avoid a fizzer, or worse, I suppose. Been drinkin', has he?' Saunders put down the blade and lifted the glass from the shelf where Deacon had placed it. He swallowed. 'Is the Scot with him?'

'Yes, sir,' said Deacon. 'They are both in K.L., both sober. What is more relative, perhaps, is the fact that they have captured a singer.'

Saunders raised an eyebrow, and put down the brush.

'What's the name of the singer? Would it be Tony Mafan?'

'Yes.'

'Mafan knows little. I've had him under observation for bloody weeks. Tony Mafan isn't a big feller. He operates a closed cell. Campbell had no damned right to go crashin' in on one of my contacts, don't you know.'

'Mafan has named *his* contact.'

'What contact?' said Saunders. 'What name did he peddle?'

'Kekao.'

'The printer. Yes, I know about Kekao, too.'

'Why haven't you questioned these people, Colonel?'

'I have. I spoke personally with Kekao.'

'And yet they are still free to buy and sell information?'

'This is a free society, more or less,' said the colonel, returning to his shaving. 'I could scratch a case for imprisonment against Mafan and his sisters, no doubt, but it wouldn't give me Kekao, and it wouldn't give me a lead to the bastard Chinkie who supplies Sand Shan with finance and arms.'

'How can you be so certain?'

Saunders tapped the side of his nose with the flat of the razor. 'Years of experience.'

Deacon said, 'Are you never wrong, Colonel?'

'Never.'

'Tony Mafan has named the Fat Cat.'

The blade stopped against the copper's foamy jaw. He swivelled his head round. 'Mafan can't possibly know. If he did, he'd never—'

'Buz Campbell has a very persuasive manner, Colonel Saunders.'

'Where are they?'

'In K.L. In a police sub-station in the Treacher Street area.'

'Campbell took Mafan in?'

'Apparently the prisoner required medical attention.'

'God of my fathers!' Saunders exclaimed. 'Your bloody fool of a sergeant *has* gone rogue.'

'Will you sanction a police vehicle with escort to bring my lads, and Mafan, back here? You can obtain jurisdiction over the prisoner if you wish to, Colonel.'

Saunders lifted a towel from the rail and swabbed dried soap from his face. 'Mafan named the Fat Cat?'

'Yes, sir. Campbell believes he told the truth.'

'Did Campbell, by any chance, leak this name to you?'

'The man's name is King. Chung Lee King. He's a businessman, owner of a shoe factory in K.L., and a couple of tin-mines up-country.'

'By God! King! That loud-mouthed, flashy Nationalist. I can't hardly believe it.'

'Do you mean Mafan is lying?'

'I mean, Mafan might be telling the truth,' said Saunders.

'Do we bring them back?'

'Not bloody likely.' Saunders brushed past Deacon on his way to the telephone. 'We get down there, toot-bloody-sweet.'

'We?'

'Inform Major Beasley I'll be needing your services.'

'For how long, Colonel?'

'For as long as it takes to haul in the net.'

If Deacon had hoped for a dramatic move against Sand Shan's organisation, he was doomed to disappointment, though Colonel Saunders did take action, rapid action at that, on the strength of the high-grade information that young Tony Mafan yielded up so liberally.

Whisked out of Treacher Street and installed in a holding cell in a special Police wing in the old Market Exchange building near the red and white mosque of Masjid Jame, Tony was treated with the care due an important prisoner. His hands plastered, a turban of bandages around his head, he looked quite pathetic, particularly as he had to depend upon brisk little Malay policemen to do practically everything for him. Wholeheartedly, Tony flung himself into the role of squealer. His encounter with Buz Campbell and the Scot had scared him badly. Until that incident, he had always assumed that all Britishers were hamstrung by honour and decency. But the sergeant with the Canadian accent was a living rebuttal of Tony's misconception. In a better world, under different circumstances, Tony would have been happy to have his kid sister married off to a guy like Campbell. But it was too late for Susu, and Tony had other things on his mind, like saving Ma and Lily from retribution and getting away with his neck.

Hard bargaining didn't begin until Saunders entered the Market Exchange building a half-hour before midnight. By that time, Colonel Saunders had met with Sergeant Campbell and Corporal McNair. Campbell, not in the least intimidated by the colonel's anger, was sunk in a disconsolate mood, too damned worn out to care.

Armed with a headful of facts, Colonel Saunders entered the interview room alone. He remained with Tony Mafan throughout the night, sending out for tea a couple of times and leaving the room once to relieve himself. It was close to dawn before Saunders summoned a stenographer from the administration office and led the weary young prisoner through a summary of statement. That done, the colonel returned Mafan to the safe-keeping of the Kuala Lumpur Police Department and collected Jeff Deacon from the cot cell in which the captain had been catching up on his sleep.

'How good is Mafan's information?' Deacon asked.

'First class. Grade one stuff, no doubt about it.'

'Did you have to squeeze him?'

Saunders said, 'No, I was kindness itself. More than the little squirt deserves, don't you know.'

Deacon said, 'Word will be out about Mafan's arrest. I doubt if Campbell and McNair were terribly discreet.'

'I've taken precautions,' said Saunders. 'I had the mother and sister picked up soon after they left work. They're being looked after in the military hospital three streets from here.'

'Hospital?'

'There's nothing wrong with them. I just want them kept cool until I get around to questionin' them.'

'And the rest of Mafan's contacts?'

'We'll pull Kekao and his staff in first thing tomorrow.'

'Are you confident that Kekao won't skip?'

'He's at home, as it happens.'

'All right,' said Deacon. 'Now tell me, if you will, about the big man on the mountain.'

'King. Yes,' said Saunders. 'It's going to be tricky to patch a case against King on the strength of Mafan's evidence. Oh, Mafan will swear all sorts of things. He'd perjure himself blue in the face for tickets to Hong Kong and three fake passports.

Unfortunately, when it comes down to it, Mafan's evidence is mostly hearsay.'

'But you do believe him?'

'He isn't lying. It's King who's behind Shan all right. King's the quartermaster, the money shark. King receives funds from a source inside China. He buys from the American black market, running guns and stores down from Korea. Been doing it for months, Mafan claims.'

'How does Mafan know all this?'

'Same as he knows about troop movements and the programme of patrols of your boys in the SAS. Mafan is smarter than anybody gave him credit for. Don't think that petty crooks like Mafan owe allegiance only to the commies. Types like Mafan would just as readily peddle information to our side.'

'Did he tell you how King operates, how King and Shan make contact?'

'He told me all he could on that score, enough to suggest that we can nab Shan, if we're slippy.'

'Shan?' Deacon's eyes gleamed. 'Lay hold of Shan?'

'Mafan claims he can pinpoint the camps.'

'Really?'

Saunders gave a dry laugh. He did not seem displeased with his night's work. He said, 'Far as I'm concerned, I'm just investigatin' a series of brutal murders. I wouldn't have jumped in with both feet if it hadn't been for your blitherin' idiot of a sergeant. But now the ball's rollin', I intend to keep it in motion.'

'You still haven't explained, Colonel, how it is that a minion like Tony Mafan can surrender the locations of Sand Shan's camps. We've never bagged anyone who could – or who would.'

Saunders said, 'It's the sister. Not Susu, the one called Lily. A common little factoryhand by day, but by night . . .'

'I see,' said Deacon. 'Mafan pimps for the guerrillas. Is that it?'

'In a nutshell. The sister Lily, plus other members of Tony Mafan's female family tree, are what our American cousins would call "party girls".'

'Does Tony take them out to the bandit camps, personally?'

'God, no. But he quizzes the girls closely when they come home.'

'You have Lily Mafan in a cell, don't you?'

'And I will be askin' that little lady a lot of serious questions, you can be certain,' said Saunders. 'Though Tony's already given me ninety per cent of the answers.'

'Look, Colonel,' said Deacon, 'I don't wish to seem like an arch-pessimist, but isn't Lee King going to go to ground as soon as he learns that we've swooped on Mafan and Kekao?'

'I thought of that,' said Saunders. 'Can't answer your question, Jeffrey. But it's my guess that we have a fightin' chance of catchin' King unprepared. Lee King may not be aware of just how *much* Mafan can divulge.'

'Well,' said Deacon, 'I wouldn't be inclined to tarry too long, Colonel.'

'I won't. That's why I'm sendin' you and your rogue NCOs back to Port Kernan. I want the cooperation of the SAS on this particular sortie.'

'Sortie?'

'The big axe,' said Saunders. 'Chop, chop, chop.'

'A coordinated series of strikes?'

'Yes.'

'But it takes time to work teams into the jungle.'

'I want them in fast,' said Saunders.

'But . . . but how?'

'That's your problem,' the copper declared.

Out of necessity, the Beezer delegated responsibility for the selection of teams to Tim Dalinart. Under the circumstances, Tim broached the task with relish. Angered by the bandits' sneak attacks, the officers and men of the SAS squadrons were raring to go.

It was rumoured that the Deke had returned from Kuala Lumpur with high-grade information and a map which purported to pinpoint Shan's camps. But the Deke wouldn't be drawn on how he had acquired the treasure. It was around the map, though, that the SAS raids were planned. Five guerrilla camps were located in or close to villages stretching in a sickle shape from the Lower Perak to the Selangor. Two lay fairly close to Kuala Lumpur. From this evidence, it seemed that the remote encampment at Totan had been Shan's main training ground. All the others were strategically situated for raids on road and rail communications and strikes against tin mines and rubber plantations.

In consultation with Deacon and other jungle veterans, Dalinart selected three teams of twenty-four men each. Police back-up had been promised. All that the SAS required to do now was wait. Go-ahead for the operation depended on what sort of information Colonel Saunders could wheedle from his crop of prisoners in Kuala Lumpur.

Buz Campbell had gone into his shell. He was neither proud nor ashamed of what he had done or of his carelessness with Susu. He said nothing, nothing at all, and went morosely about his tasks brushing aside all expressions of sympathy from fellow NCOs.

'Is he all right, P.B.?' Deacon asked the Scot.

'Aye. He just wants t' kill somebody, that's all.'

Beasley had not returned from Singapore when Saunders turned up in Port Kernan again.

Number One Copper was jubilant.

He took over the major's office and summoned Tim Dalinart and Deacon to an immediate pow-wow late on Sunday evening. Deacon had been about to take off for dinner at the St John's, his first off-duty spell since the massacre, but telephoned Allison and cancelled. What Saunders had in mind would not wait.

'Close the door, Jeffrey,' Saunders said.

Tim Dalinart was already seated, not on the major's chair but on a three-legged stool in a corner, as if he was in disgrace. It was breathlessly hot that night and Tim sought a draught from the gridded window behind its rattan screen. Deacon pulled out a chair and seated himself, too.

'I won't beat around the bush,' said Saunders. 'We've got him.'

'Shan or Lee King, sir?' asked Tim Dalinart.

'If we're fast and have a bit of luck, we'll have both of them,' Saunders answered.

'Go on, Colonel,' said Deacon.

'It appears everybody has a crumb of information they shouldn't have about Lee King. He's big man on the mountain, and no mistake. We always knew that. A member of the Inter-continental Club, the Malayan Mining Association, contributor to the best native charities. Big *respectable* chap. Rich too, and not shy about showing it. Never the hint of a blemish against him.'

'Really?' said Dalinart.

'Well, a faint hint here and there,' Saunders admitted. 'But the girl, the sister of Tony Mafan, she knew a lot about our Mr King. Street gossip. God of my fathers, it's a sorry state of affairs when every little tart knows more about the true state of things than the police.'

'Did the girl give information voluntarily?' asked Deacon.

'Oh, quite voluntarily,' said Saunders. 'I let her have a chat with her brother. Tony managed to persuade her that it was time for the family to start a new life in Hong Kong.'

'She did a deal?'

'She ain't clever enough to do a deal. She's no Mata Hari,' said Saunders. 'But she had a lot of valuable information floatin' about in that head of hers. She put me on to a driver named Mao Tan, an old Chink who runs a taxi service and, it turns out, is on the pay-roll of King himself. Understand, we're not at the top of the tree or anywhere near it. I couldn't patch a case out of what I've got so far. Particularly as witnesses like Mao Tan would sing dumb if I got them within a mile of a court.'

'Can you connect Shan and King?'

'Peking is the connection. King is Shan's contact with Peking. What I want is to catch the pair of them together. They do meet from time to time. King isn't just quartermaster for the guerrillas. Shan and he discuss targets. Shan's more or less told what to do.'

'Skating round the Malayan Communist Party, do you mean?'

'It's speculation, really,' said Saunders. 'But, yes, that's what it smells like. Sand Shan's killer squads are an independent arm of Chinese aggression. Vicious and unscrupulous. The "new soldiers" of communism.'

'And the American weapons?'

'A bonus,' said Saunders. 'I don't know how or from whom King makes his black-market buys but the Americans have somebody who's selling out his country for money, too.'

'Malaya isn't the Americans' war,' said Dalinart. 'Free enterprise will always rule.'

'Be that as it may,' Saunders went on, 'if I can catch King red-handed in the company of Sand Shan, then I'll have him dead to rights. What's more, he'll do any sort of deal I care to name. The rich ones are always easy meat. King won't want to forfeit his fat bank accounts and serve a ten-stretch in a penal colony.'

'I assume you didn't extract all this information from Mafan's sister,' said Dalinart.

' 'Course not. She provided names and places. She didn't realise how valuable the data was. Amazin' how many small fry we picked up around K.L. Like the taxi driver and Kekao. Come to think of it, the entire guerrilla movement in Malaya is made up of small fry.' Saunders paused, then said, 'I also bagged a coolie who had worked for a while as Shan's radio operator.'

Deacon's interest was immediate. 'Did you, now?'

'Obviously this chap didn't have a complete picture of what was going on, but he travelled with Shan for six months or so.'

'Why did he give up?' asked Tim Dalinart. 'Don't bandit radio ops earn lots of dollars?'

'Oh, domestic trouble. His wife was carryin' on with another bloke, that sort of story. He was up-country most of the time. He didn't like the jungle life. He was Shanghai stock, a city-boy, born and bred.'

'I'm surprised Shan let him go.'

'He ran off.'

'Where did you find him?'

'Out near Batu – without the faithless wife. He bedded Lily Mafan from time to time. Paid her. He was into smuggling, which is why he was less than happy when me and my lads turned up on his doorstep at the crack of dawn.'

'He's being cooperative, is he?'

'Extra polite,' said Saunders.

'Can we use him?'

'Can't we, though?' said Saunders.

The police chief unrolled a map of the Central Peninsula on the desk top. He pinned it down at the corners with objects from the drawer. The major and the captain peered over his shoulders.

'This, I've deduced, is how the system works,' said Saunders. 'The big convoy – the one you lot intercepted – didn't come from one place. It started out from three different centres and merged in the foothills, here. It supplied the permanent camp at the Totan, which was not, I've learned, Shan's pigeon at all, but was under the command of Kwai Yan Chung.'

'Is that where he trained his killer squads?'

'It's certainly where he got his raw material from.'

'Where does Shan hole out?' Tim Dalinart asked.

'In one of these three small villages,' said Saunders.

'So close to K.L.?'

'Not all that close,' said Saunders.

'You've been very busy, Colonel.'

'Not all that busy, either,' said Saunders. 'And not 'arf as busy as I'm going to be.'

'Do you, by any chance, intend to arrange a meeting between Shan and King?'

'Bingo, Jeff! No silly waitin' around. Shan's got too many spies in the country. I'm hangin' on to the radio op like grim death. I have him tucked away in a nice quiet room not ten miles from K.L.'

'Safe, I hope,' said Deacon.

'An honoured guest,' said Saunders. 'But as secure as a bank vault. Most of the others, I released, including Kekao. Lee King is now well aware that we've a purge on. I mean, blast it, Shan and King couldn't have expected anything else after the Port Kernan massacre.'

'And Shan?'

'He travels with a handful of men. Sometimes only a pair, disguised as simple paddi farmers. If he requires a meet with Lee King, he calls through to King's radio contact.'

'At the tin mine?'

'The tin mine is temporarily closed,' said Saunders. 'That's something that didn't show up in local reports. Why the devil didn't I have a patrol up there before now? I'm getting past it, perhaps. In any case, it's just as well I didn't spookify Mr King. Shan and he are probably still of the impression that the tin mine, their meeting-place, is safe.'

'I like it very much,' said Deacon. 'Will it work, however? Is there no special code or signal that Shan uses when he wants to summon a meet?'

'Yes. But our renegade radio op knows what it is – unless it's been changed, of course.'

'Is that the random factor?' said Tim Dalinart.

'That's it,' said Saunders. 'I'm not a miracle worker. I can't cover every eventuality.'

'We slip the radio op into the area,' said Deacon, 'and send two separate messages on the correct wavelengths to Shan and to King asking for a meet. What if they acknowledge, each to the other?'

'Do you know what a "jammer" is?'

'Absolutely,' said Deacon.

'Well, we'll simply block out their radios after we pass the fake messages.'

Dalinart glanced at Jeff Deacon. 'What do you think?'

'I think it sounds fine,' said Deacon. 'I doubt if it's foolproof but nothing is in this war. The theory, Colonel Saunders, is excellent and you are to be congratulated on it.'

Saunders nodded. Praise was no more than his due. He tapped his forefinger on the map. 'Shan will come down the

Tennga Valley from one of these three hide-outs. It's the only possible route for him, unless he grows wings and flies and he don't appear to have a 'copter at his disposal any longer. So – down the Tennga Valley to a rendezvous at the Dejur, this old gravel-pump tin mine.'

'Have you been to the location, Colonel?'

'I thought it best to steer clear.'

'A recce would be very useful.'

'I have photographs.'

Dalinart said, 'Believe it or not, I've been there – what? – a year ago. With Pawson, on a swing patrol. Limestone hills back on to the mine area but the jungle's grown in again between the mine and K.L., though, obviously, there's still a fairly decent road and a railway line.'

'What's the terrain like behind the hills?' Deacon enquired.

'Thick palm-type jungle. The limestone faults out along a ridge. Lots of water. Lots of dense undergrowth, if I recall. The usual green rubbish.'

'Is the tin mine completely deserted?' Deacon said.

The colonel answered, 'Lee King keeps on a maintenance crew. Roughly a dozen men. Apparently the veins or "pipes" of tin in the limestone aren't worked out yet.'

'Why did the mine stop producing?'

Saunders shrugged. 'Perhaps it was more valuable for other purposes.'

'All right,' said Deacon. 'Let's regard the area as the centre of a sweep.'

'Marching fire?' said Dalinart.

'Approximately that sort of manoeuvre, yes,' said Deacon. 'What I propose to do is this, Colonel, with your permission . . .'

'Show us,' said Saunders.

Deacon drew the map across the desk and the three men bent over it.

'We'll send in SAS teams drawn from 'A' Squadron against the marked camps, getting them as close as possible to the targets by jeep, and using fast march in on the villages.'

'Secure all Shan's bolt-holes?'

'Exactly,' said Deacon. 'It needn't be done to a rigid time-plan and it need not be done with great stealth. In other words, it doesn't matter if Shan learns that there is a jungle purge against him. He'll be on his way through the Tennga Valley, on down to the Dejur Mine, by that time. We'll make quite certain that we do not scorch his tail-feathers.'

'Sound enough so far, Jeff.'

'I'll be positioned in the Valley, with a small team, a very small team. Once Shan comes through, I'll move my team up close to the mine and close the back door. 'A' Squadron will be here, twenty-odd miles to the north-east. The moment Shan steps into the Valley, they start to travel cross-country. Back-up, in other words.'

'Got it,' said Saunders. 'You'll want me and my coppers to let Lee King through, then close the escape routes on the K.L. side of Dejur?'

'That's it,' said Deacon. 'Once Shan and King are together in the mine building, they are trapped. We close and bolt the doors on them. Fling police and security troops around the area, and move in.'

'What if Shan elects to shoot it out?' asked Saunders. 'I want the pair of them alive.'

'It isn't Shan's style. Even if he wants to, however, I question if Lee King would buy that one. King will still be hoping to bargain and bribe his way out of trouble.'

Dalinart nodded. 'It seems a first-class plan to me, Jeff. What do you say to it, Colonel Saunders?'

'I say – yes.'

'How soon can we move?' asked Deacon.

'Almost immediately,' said Saunders. 'But I have one question, something you obviously haven't thought of, Jeff.'

'What's that?'

'How are you going to get a team, even a small team, high into the jungles of the Tennga Valley, without rousing the bandits?'

'Yes,' said Dalinart, frowning, 'and in a matter of a day. It's virtually impossible, Jeff.'

'No, it isn't,' said Deacon. 'I intend to go in by air.'

'Parachute?' said Saunders.

'Why not?'

'Into the trees?' said Dalinart.

'Into the trees,' said Deacon.

'But para-dropping directly into the trees has never been done before.'

'So much the better,' said Deacon.

'Will I organise a practice jump?' asked Dalinart.

'Under no circumstances,' said Deacon.

Allison was told nothing of the nature of the operation. It was not Deacon's way to burden her with speculations. The less she knew of the details of his 'work' with the SAS, the better for her peace of mind. It was not that he did not trust her. Even with the salutary lesson of Susu Mafan to the fore, Deacon would have trusted Allison Wingfield with his life. Besides, Allison hated the communists, Shan in particular, almost as much as Deacon did. It was not a good thing to carry an excess of hatred into battle. It diminished perspective, made one unduly rash. There was nothing rash in SAS planning. They were merely adventurous, experimental and courageous. The planning would be meticulous. Tim Dalinart would see to that. The RAF pilot who would ferry Deacon's team over the limestone hills of the Tennga would be the best in the business. The equipment would be checked and rechecked and Tim would even have a scale model of the dropping-zone made up in the garrison workshops, working from aerial photographs which Saunders had supplied and from large-scale maps.

Before Deacon left to take dinner with Allison at the St John's Hotel in the Port, the teams from 'A' Squadron were already drawing kit and moving towards the muster-hut for final briefing and despatch. Transport, in the form of three-ton trucks and armoured jeeps, was revving up in the pool and the arc-lights which squared the Port Kernan garrison blazed.

Major Beasley would have loved it all, would have provided a last ounce of ginger needed to bring the troopers to an absolute peak; but the Beezer had been unable to return from Singapore in time for the commencement of the operation, though his approval for it and his sanction had been sought, and he had checked it through with the Joint Security Staff and argued the case for immediate action.

The massacre at the Paradise Gardens seemed to have happened ages ago, though the dead of the regiment had been buried only yesterday. Deacon had stood by the gravesides, listening to the bugle calls, the crack of rifle salvos, with a feeling in his heart that this might be his last salute too, that more than the bodies of the dead were being interred in the red Malayan earth.

When Allison and he were alone in the bed in the opulent suite in the St John's, lying side by side, Deacon said, 'If we went back to England, what would we do?'

'Besides this, you mean?' said Allison, then sensing his gravity, apologised. 'I'm sorry, darling. I didn't mean to be flippant. But the possibility of going home is rather remote.'

'Perhaps not,' said Deacon.

'Do you mean you'd consider applying for a transfer at the end of your tour?'

'No, not that. Quitting altogether.'

The woman said nothing for a moment.

Deacon too was silent.

From far below came restrained music from the hotel's ballroom, though there were few guests there that night.

It was early, not yet ten o'clock. In London, young gentlemen of Deacon's class would be starting out 'on the town', finishing dinner or settling into their seats for the last acts of West End plays. Austerity would not deter them from enjoying themselves. To most people in Britain, Malaya must seem remote, the 'emergency' there, nothing but a colonial skirmish.

Before dawn, before the sun broke over the hills of the Tennga Valley, however, Deacon and Buz Campbell and Corporal McNair would be plunging out of the belly of a low-flying Valetta airplane and landing in the spear-like trees. Before another day had passed, they would be engaged in fighting of some sort, with Bren and Sten and bayonet. By nightfall tomorrow it was possible that one or all of them would be dead. There would be an obituary in the *Times*, a few lines in the *Guardian*, but by their very nature, the men of the Special Air Service would not be praised as heroes. They would die secretly, with secretive honour, to keep the distant peninsulas and islands of the world free from tyranny.

On the night before battle, there was no heroism, no premonitions and precious little room for thoughts of honour. You were a man in bed with a woman, and had the future before you.

Deacon said, 'Would we be happy?'

Allison said, 'I imagine I could learn to live without orchids and humidity and the smell of cinnamon trees.'

'And lizards and the *Straits Times* and—'

'And never quite knowing if you are going to come back.'

Deacon paused, then said, 'Yes, of course.'

'It isn't soldiering, Jeff. It's fighting, that's what you do, and I'm frightened.'

'I might be rather a dull old dog without it.'

'At least you'd stand a chance of becoming old,' said Allison. 'Don't you see, there's no end to it for men like you? No end except . . .'

Deacon murmured, 'It had occurred to me, you know.'

'Is this it? Is this the last push?'

'Come what may, yes. Between Saunders and our chaps, yes, this time we will destroy him. Shan, I mean.'

And all the other Sand Shans?'

'I'll leave them to my heirs.'

'How generous!' said Allison.

'Isn't it?'

'Do you know where Shan is?'

'Not exactly. We intend to lure him out into the open.'

'How long will it take?'

'Not too long,' said Deacon. 'It should be interesting.'

'Interesting is hardly the word.'

'This time, Allison, when it's over, we'll talk about an end to fighting. About going home again.'

‘I hope it isn’t too late, Jeff.’

Deacon put his arm around her and drew her against his body.

He hugged her gently, thinking of other things, particularly of Shan. Thinking, too, of the parachute drop, that commitment to luck which no soldier liked; riding the tiger.

‘Jeff.’ Her mouth was against his chest. He could feel her lips move against his flesh. ‘Jeff, do you really mean it?’

‘Yes,’ he answered. ‘I mean it. I really, really mean it.’

In the empty ballroom three floors below, the sad string quartet had surrendered to apathy and were playing *God Save The King*.

Riding the tiger

The method most commonly used to extract tin from alluvial deposits, especially in the section of the industry owned by Chinese businessmen, was by gravel-pumping. Dredging was big-scale stuff and confined to corporations and international combines. But the investment required to establish a gravel-pumping mine was comparatively modest, and Chinese immigrants had been quick to seize on it as a potentially solid venture. Gravel-pump mines required a heavy labour force, however, and had a short life span. The regions of the Central belt, which had seen the biggest expansion in mining in the years between the wars, were pock-marked with the 'long graves' of worked-out diggings. Shrewd operators – and Lee King was one of them – kept their mines open, however, and operated at a loss. Complete closure would mean that the mine would have to be flooded and the State development grant brought under scrutiny. It was cheaper to keep the Dejur open than to abandon it. If tin prices continued to rise, then Lee King could go into production again. Even a very low yield of tin-concentrate would push the operation back into profit.

Except for its location and the bizarre shape of the backing hill of limestone which guillotined off the throat of the valley, the Dejur was much the same in appearance as any small tin mine. There was a branch-head pipe which carried volumes of water to the high-pressure heads of monitor nozzles whose jets broke up the ore-bearing ground. The resulting slurry, thick as gruel, flowed into sumps from whence it was sucked up by the pumps and vomited into *palongs* or sluices. They were sloped to allow the material to flow over baffles. The baffles gathered the tin-ore which was washed out against an inflowing stream of clean water, while the waste was flushed out into a tailings area close to the ridge where it formed a series of shallow ponds.

The twelve employees who remained at Dejur were experienced tin-miners and knew how to use the equipment. They were also communist sympathisers. Their job was to keep the mine in working order. This they did by running the nozzles and *palongs* for an hour or so every three or four days, and by keeping the equipment clean and oiled. Tin-ore was gathered in minute quantities and stored, undressed, in wooden wagons. As the Dejur had been closed for many months, the gathered product didn't amount to much and certainly didn't justify use of the rail-line. Instead, a tip-truck removed the ore every couple of months; a large eight-wheeled American job with a diesel engine, and a comfortable cabin which could hold three men in addition to the driver.

It was in the Mack tip-truck that Mr King made his periodic trips from Kuala Lumpur along the bumpy, overgrown road to the Dejur Mine. The Mercedes sedan which preceded the Mack was a blind, a decoy. Mr Lee King was a very cautious man.

The employees resident at Dejur had their own transport, a couple of beat-up Ford vans and one old jeep. They came into K.L. every so often to pick up stores and to cash-out the wage chits which they had accumulated. Now and then they returned to Dejur with a whole lot more than fresh fruit and a handful of dollars. Once every two months or so they smuggled back a crate of Made-in-USA rifles, a box of hand-grenades or anti-personnel mines or plastic explosive. Occasionally a strong steel box full of hard cash would be handed over to a youthful-looking man with glasses, who would appear out of the jungle, accompanied by a small band of guerrillas. The young man with glasses wore no military insignia and the lads at the Dejur had no reason to suppose that this was the legendary Wei Sand Shan in person.

Smart lads in Military Intelligence or the inner enclaves of Police HQ were equally dumb when it came to Wei Sand Shan. It is doubtful if even those who had worked on his dossier for years would have recognised him immediately. There were no known photographs of Sand Shan, who had apparently been 'camera-shy' since childhood. Artist-drawn likenesses did not capture the boyishness, the slightness of the bandit leader. Sand

Shan did not behave like a warlord. Of all the men in Malaya opposed to the communist cause, only one could be certain of recognising Sand Shan on sight. Absolutely certain. His name was Jeffrey Alexander Deacon.

Wei Sand Shan hardly glanced up through the palms which surrounded the tiny village of Lautti, a settlement of aboriginal tribesmen, Chinese squatters and bandits, as the fat-bellied Valetta droned overhead, its shape only just visible in the first pale flush of dawn. And Jeffrey Alexander Deacon, crouched by the exit hatch within the aircraft, did not look down.

Single transports were a common sight across the defile of the Tennga Valley and the heel of the Selangor, and gave no cause for anxiety. There was no clear ground of any kind to form a landing-strip within fifty air miles, and the RAF had no 'copters in service as yet. Sand Shan did not fear the SAS and did not anticipate close pursuit. He was much more anxious, however, when the radio operator brought him a scribbled transcript of a message that had come through from K.L. under the familiar code.

Shan did not suspect that the message might be fake. On the contrary, he had been expecting the summons. What gave rise to apprehension in Shan's cold heart was the fact that he could not quite predict how his superiors across the China Sea would react to the raid on Port Kernan. The raid had been his idea and his idea alone. He had had no time and no opportunity to make contact with Lee King and, through King's underground, with the policy-makers in Peking.

The truth was that Shan did not care what the generals in China thought of him, or whether they approved of his executions or not. But he feared, a little, that the money might dry up, that he might be reduced to begging from village to village and that his effectiveness as a rebel would be diminished. It had never occurred to Wei Sand Shan that he would lose his life in the struggle against the imperialists, only that he might become an outcast of the system under whose banner he fought and whose aims, ostensibly, he pressed on the people over whom he would eventually rule.

To be near enough K.L. for Lee King to contact him had been one reason why Shan had trekked rapidly to the miserable jungle hamlet of Lautti, by-passing the chain of 'friendly' villages between Port Kernan and Dejur on the route. Another reason was his need for cash, for enough to 'buy' back the loyalty he had sacrificed by the killing of Kwai Yan Chung and other officers and men. He would need Mr King's help in finding a suitable replacement for his second-in-command, an experienced guerrilla brought over from Shanghai, perhaps. But he would have to be wary of anyone sent by the Committee; an outsider might prove to be a usurper.

Shan read the scribbled pencil message again.

He had no need to make reply. The operator had acknowledged receipt of the message; that was always enough.

Dawn tomorrow at the Dejur.

Today he would travel south down hidden jungle trails to the blade-rock hills behind the mine. He would not wait for Mr Lee King to summon him again. He would be installed, in hiding, in Dejur before the big man arrived.

Overhead, the sky was clear now. The low growl of the Valetta's engines had waned completely away.

Hooked to the static line, the parachute bloomed above Buz Campbell soon after he cleared the door in the side of the Valetta. The sky was clear and cool but away to the east a band of blood-red cloud lowered dramatically. Stars were hard and bright as studs, the jungle lands below the sergeant's boots tar-black. The Vaughan shotgun in a quilted valise was strapped to Buz's leg. The weapon, together with a quantity of other gear, including a two-hundred-foot coil of inch-and-a-half manilla rope, sucked him fast through the air and yanked on his burly frame when the 'chute spread and filled.

There was no wind to speak of, not like there had been that long-ago night above the icy mountains of the Caucasus when a gale had ripped the SAS stick apart and fisted two transports into the rocks. Buz did not feel now as he had done then, almost ten years ago. He could still recall, in his body as well as his mind, the exhilaration of the Russian drop, that mingling of terror and excitement which made his daredevil heart pound. Then, in the prime of life, he had flirted with death in a kind of feverish rage, grappled with it willingly and eagerly. Now he carried no such vigour. He no longer cared much what happened to him. Indifference had taken over from courage. He did not even give a curt shout, a battlecry, as he thrust himself out of the plane and fell silent as a leaf towards the darkness.

P.B. was off to Buz's right, not far away, the Deke's 'chute beyond that. Buz could just make out the pale silks beyond the scalloped border. They fell nearly straight, with a slight, predictable degree of drift, while the RAF transport droned out of sight.

Up in the pine forests of northern Canada, fire-fighting teams had been perfecting this technique for the past three or four years. Buz had read of it during his term in New Orleans. He had figured it would be just the job for SAS assault patrols if ever they were again summoned to fight in the jungles of Burma. He hadn't dreamed that he would be one of the first guys in a cherry beret to try it.

He watched the tree-tops rush up to meet him.

He kept his legs loose, not braced, sitting a little in the harness. Relaxation was usually the key to a safe landing, more so when you didn't know what the fuck you were going to hit.

The jungle came closer. He could hear the pre-dawn sound of it, like a sleeper breathing, shrilling birds, chatter of monkeys. And he saw the pale trunks and the pale saddle of the palm branches below him. No sign of a clearing.

The trees were uneven in height and did not, from this weird perspective, form an unbroken canopy. It was like dropping into a stormy green sea. He was close enough to pick out individual trees, to select the clump he would aim for, thick and bushy and strong. He still didn't know what to expect, what it would feel like. A certain mild curiosity impinged on the sergeant's numbness, that paralysis he'd been feeling in heart and mind since the bomb had gone off in the Paradise.

He aimed his boots at a thick branch and rushed bodily into the skin-stripping foliage of the jungle tops.

Lower by far than he had anticipated, the branch did not halt his descent. It yielded, sprang back at him and, like a bow, shot him forwards and upwards. He had a vision of himself swan-diving all the way down to the deck. But lower branches caught him as the 'chute settled and snagged around the leaves. Enmeshed in ropes and cords and branches, the sergeant was snapped hard against the forked trunk. Given an inch less play, he might have been trapped there like a moth in a spider's web. At least he wasn't ass up. He had taken the precaution of arming himself with two knives. He got his left hand to the pocket on the thigh of his smock and drew up the cork butt of the hunting blade between finger and thumb. His right arm was painfully twisted behind his back, snared by webbing. His right thigh, back of the knee, was crooked over a branch, and his left leg, splinted by the shotgun valise, hung freely in the air. He could not look down. At least he wasn't injured. Not yet. Very cautiously and patiently, Buz fished out the knife, closed his fingers on it and, with movements of the forearm and wrist only, started to saw himself free, one strand at a time.

Some technique, jumping into the trees. Put yourself and the mission in the lap of the goddamned gods, and always would. The local fauna was ranting something friggin' awful. He sure had surprised the hell out of the denizens of the treetops. Folds of silk cascaded down over Buz and he swept them away, furling them behind him around a branch. His hips and legs were clear now and he adjusted his position until he was astride the branch. He teased the end of the coil of manilla from under the cross-straps at his chest, and secured it to the branch, laced it up with a three-foot loop and knotted himself to it. If he fell now, he would drop no more than a yard.

Christ, but it was difficult and complicated. Thank God the commies weren't prowling around below. You could be picked off at randon like a goddamned arthritic gibbon and couldn't do nothing to protect yourself, no way, no how.

Fifteen minutes later, muscles aching, Buz Campbell lowered himself one hundred and sixty feet to the floor of the forest.

Deacon and P.B. were waiting for him.

'You okay?' the Scot asked.

'Yeah, yeah.'

'What happened, Buz? Did you become entangled?'

'Right.'

'It's a dangerous manoeuvre, isn't it?' said Deacon.

Buz didn't answer. He was trying to disengage the rope. He had fixed it through a loop directly to the tree, failing to use the snaplink which had been provided for the purpose. A mistake.

'I landed half-way down the damned trunk,' said Deacon. 'It took me all my time to swing against the tree, into something solid.'

'Aye, you could break your back at this game, nae bother.'

Buz gave up on the rope. 'It's friggin' jammed.'

'P.B.,' said Deacon. 'Do you think you could shin up the tree far enough to cut the rope? Say, thirty feet or so. It's a little too obvious as it is.'

'Aye, right.'

The corporal divested himself of his pack and laid his Enfield rifle on the dry ground. He studied the swollen bole of the palm for a moment then delicately found finger and toe holds and hoisted himself on to it. Minutes later, secure among the branches, he had reached a point forty feet from the ground and, laid along a great sappy stalk, cut the manilla which fell slithering like a snake. Deacon coiled it up and stowed it in his pack.

Buz made no apology. Deacon was well aware of how risky the drop had been. The business with the rope was minor, a tiny hitch. While P.B. shinned down again, Buz unstrapped the valise from his leg and took out the Vaughan shotgun. He loaded it, clicked on the safety, and stood it against a tree, while he stuffed the soft valise into his pack. The packs, though not bulky, weighed heavy. Mostly ammunition, a little food and a half-gallon fresh water canteen apiece. If all went according to schedule, by dusk they would be within striking distance of the Dejur tin mine.

Compass and map laid out, Deacon took a bearing. No problem in route-finding. The contours ran towards the valley and the valley sloped towards the line of hills.

The light had filtered down through the leafage before the men set off, Deacon in the lead, picking stealthily downward under the tallest of the trees where the undergrowth was least dense.

It seemed strange to be on deep patrol without the Gurkha and the Dyak but Deacon had refused to bring Johnny Badhur along on this one, and the Dyak, who had no parachute experience, would have baulked at boarding an aeroplane; the prospect of flying filled him with pagan dread. P.B. reckoned he understood the Deke's reason for leaving Johnny – the Deke didn't expect them to come back. This was the last roll of the dice. Do or fuckin' die time.

Throughout the morning, the team progressed towards the head of the Tennga. They could see nothing of the way ahead, only trees. There were no vantage points, no hills to give sight-line to the limestone ridge beyond which the Dejur mine spread out under an open sky. Unmapped streams flowed sluggishly, then, later in the day, became clearer and more rapid. The region's only river was to the east, two or three miles away. By it, so trackers had told Deacon, was a path broad enough to take elephants.

The day was hot and stifling. Sweat soaked the soldiers' jungle greens, making them as wet as if they had waded through swamp. The pack-straps chafed their shoulders, making superficial sores. Black flies abounded and wild fruit trees, with fruit rotting on the boughs, were places to be avoided, strident with wasps and small but ferocious Malayan bees. By mid-afternoon, the team had come within six miles of the ridge. Deacon was driving on at a fierce pace, determined to make position before nightfall. The sky, what they could glimpse of it, was the hue of tarnished brass.

Buz was labouring. Oldest of the three, and worn by the

strain of the past month, he seemed to maintain pace by sheer willpower. Big shoulders swinging, he looked more like a grizzled mountain-bear than ever. Even P.B. was having trouble. His back and thighs screamed for rest. The Enfield rifle had swollen to the size and weight of a tree trunk in his hands. The flesh of his hands was scalded with the salt sweat and the flicking cuts of grasses and leaves.

Somewhere to the left, in an easterly direction, three other SAS teams were suffering the same sort of hell. But probably not at this killing pace. They would be set to a march rate, spurred on by Pawson or Hornby or Dalinart, since the major had elected to climb into this raid himself. One or more of the teams would be bound to have encountered resistance. It was part of their brief to take and temporarily secure the native villages which lay along the route. Chances were that Shan would have men there. By now, several of the squadron might be dead, others wounded. Luck of the draw, mate. Bloody queer how you were forced to operate in this devil-ridden country. No war this for parade-ground soldiers. Perhaps they were the last of the old breed, the bandits of the British army. P.B. tried to recapture some swagger, the feeling of bravado which had been so good during the Nazi war. But it was gone, gone for good and gone for ever. Like Buz, he felt defeated, almost doomed. Finally, with the cloud lid pressed down and the smell of thunder sizzling in the oppressive air, the SAS troops reached their spot point.

The jungle-clad ridge reared before them. The trees on the valley bed thinned enough to give them sight of it. It looked high as an alp, though the crest was no more than four hundred feet above sea-level and most of it lay below three hundred. Cloud clung to the trees like the dusty webs of many spiders, motionless and still. There was no rain yet, however, and the air was so thick you could feel it going down into your lungs like broth.

They put up the first animals they had encountered all day. Four buffalo, sensing the presence of men, trampled off into the shelter of thorn scrub.

Deacon came to a halt. He leaned his pack against a tree trunk. Buz staggered and almost fell. He let himself sink to one knee, breath sawing in his throat. Only P.B. managed to hold himself upright. With familiar nonchalance, he lit a cigarette and smoked it with the butt curled into his fist to hide the glow. He dispersed smoke gently with a flap of his wrist. The tobacco tasted rotten in his sticky throat.

Deacon said, 'The Dejur Mine is just over the ridge. We'll have to climb.'

Both soldiers had known that they would avoid the path; it came as no shock.

Deacon said, 'I want the position before dusk, and in this light it'll be dark in a couple of hours.'

'What are we waitin' for, then?' said P.B.

'Move quietly,' said Deacon. 'There may be look-outs positioned on the ridge. One can never tell what Shan will do.'

But the slopes of the limestone hill hid no guerrillas or sentries from the Dejur Mine, none, that is, that the three SAS men could detect.

The head of the Tennga Valley was not high enough for there to be much change in the nature of the forest, though, on the ramps of the ridge itself, oak and laurel had found root among the primitive vegetation. With the last dregs of energy, Buz and P.B. clawed and crawled after the captain, who selected a meandering course towards the ridge crest, avoiding the thickest of the scrub and the need to blaze trail with *parangs*. Noises might echo out of the jungle, caught and amplified by tusk-like escarpments which jutted from the green stuff near the summit. For all Deacon knew, the chop of a steel blade on bark might reach the ears of the communists at the Dejur as loudly as a coconut drum. The closer he came to the funnel of the valley and to the mine beyond, the more tense and nervous Deacon became. Detection at this stage would blow the operation, though it would not necessarily put them in risk of their lives.

As the men climbed, often on hands and knees, the earth lost its spongy softness and became dry and crumbly. At long last, the undergrowth thinned, spanning into individual trees, palms and gnarled pines. Stealth and haste did not meld well and Deacon, too, was drained by the long day's march. When finally he reached the rolling summit, where the ridge folded towards open country, Deacon flopped on his belly and laid his head on his hands for two or three minutes, recovering strength.

Buz and P.B. straggled up beside him and flopped, too, in a grassy saddle between two rocks.

By good luck rather than navigational skill, Deacon had brought them out at an ideal vantage point. From the shelter of the limestone they could scan the area of the Dejur workings and, more important, have full view of the jungle track which emerged from a narrow pass three hundred feet below.

The captain sucked from his canteen, which he had filled at the last stream, doctoring the contents with a couple of purifying tablets. The water tasted metallic and unpleasant but his body, his cells, craved liquid and he gulped mouthful after mouthful as sweat oozed from his pores, then, swiftly, cooled. He mopped his face and neck with his beret and lifted himself forward while P.B. slipped off his pack.

Armed with a monocular lens, Deacon rowed himself on hands and knees through the scattered rocks and settled on his stomach again.

There was no depth to the sky, no indication that the sun was setting. Cloud flattened all perspectives, cloud of dull brownish olive and texture of prison distemper. Away to the west, thunder snarled. A brief, whisking sheen of electric blue light showed where sheet-lightning flashed over the Strait of Malacca. A hot breeze, like air from a furnace vent, dispersed the mists from the ridge. Deacon's fingers trembled in the aftermath of physical effort. He held the lens steady with both hands and delicately adjusted focus.

For fifteen minutes he remained in a prone position, studying the lie of the terrain, the setting of the mine. Two long sheds were lighted. Men came and went about one of them, obviously domestic quarters. A wireless released cheap jazz music every time the door opened. No dogs were visible around the place, though. After all, the skeleton crew at Dejur had nothing to fear from bandits. In rapidly diminished light, Deacon tried to take in as many details as possible, to imprint them on his memory. Tomorrow they would have to be off the ridge before daylight.

The path from the jungle emerged through a narrow corridor at the base of the ridge. Somebody had cleared and planted the ground there, though it had recently gone back to rank grass. You could discern the shape of the track through the paddi, to the spot by a lumber pile where it wandered on to an apron of beaten earth near the tailings.

There was water in the tailings, perhaps only mud. From here it resembled lime jelly, slick and static. The only glimmer of motion came from the gate of the sluice at the bend of the stream where the current was turned into the workings and led by a series of canals to the pump reservoir. There was nobody out in the workings. Pumps and nozzles were silent. It was almost dark. Lights in the sheds showed plain, like stencils cut from the papery air.

Apart from the width of open ground, and the cover it provided, wedge-shaped Dejur, backed by ridges, formed a perfect trap.

Deacon started as P.B. nuzzled alongside him.

'What d'you think, Deke?' P.B. whispered.

'It looks highly promising. Where's Buz?'

'Havin' a nap.'

'Really?'

'He's knackered,' said P.B. 'Be all right on the night, though.'

Deacon handed P.B. the glass. 'There, to the right. That's the exit from the valley. A single track. There's no other way to the mine. If Shan comes at all, he'll come along that path.'

'What if he arrives durin' the night?'

'Assuming Saunders got the messages right,' said Deacon, 'the meet isn't scheduled until daybreak. But, yes, Shan's devilish cunning. He may well slip close to the sheds under cover of darkness.'

'We'll need to get closer, then.'

'I agree,' said Deacon, hand covering mouth. 'We'll rest up until midnight, then wriggle down a couple of hundred feet or so. Do you see the clump by the jagged rock there?'

'Stuff looks like cactus?'

'Yes,' said Deacon. 'We'll try to take position there. If Shan moves through that grass tonight, we'll hear him.'

'Why don't we go now?'

'Too visible,' said Deacon. 'Besides, we might be heard.'

'Aye, right. I wish we'd brought a couple dozen of the lads wi' us. We could've sealed yon place off proper.'

'Can you imagine a large team making it this far without being spotted?' said Deacon. 'Saunders will have a full police platoon, armed and keen as mustard, at his command, come morning.'

P.B. nodded and handed the glass back to Deacon.

Deacon sat up a little. The sky to the west flared again and the howitzer boom of thunder grew louder.

'Storm on the way,' Deacon said. 'We had best eat and rest while we can.'

'No lights?' P.B. asked.

'No lights,' said Deacon.

The rain began around eight p.m. It preceded the thunderstorm by a quarter of an hour. On the ridge the trees gave shelter for only a short period of time. The rain increased to a deluge which battered even the largest leaves and bent the stalks and flooded the crumbling limestone hollows within minutes. It wasn't only the volume of soaking, cold water which slashed down out of the heavens that made things miserable for the SAS trio, the sounds of the tropical storm prowling rapidly towards them played havoc with the imagination. Even men who had spent umpteen hours under pounding guns and had survived battles galore were awed by the ferocity of the weather. The hill was split by brilliant lightning. Thunder caught your guts and wrenched them. There was no escape. Peal followed peal into a continuous explosive reverberation. Stark flashes lit the trees, lit the rods of rain as blasts of wind smote the funnel of the Tennga Valley. Oak, laurel, pine and palm were whipped by the sudden hurricane.

Huddled in oilskin capes, the three SAS men crouched against the limestone rocks. Buz drew his head under the hood of the cape. P.B. could not bear to watch the lightning and pressed his beret to his eyes with both fists. Only Deacon kept watch through the worst of the storm. Hands visored across his forehead, he peered at the mine workings in the sharp blue glare until tails of rain wiped them out.

Common sense told the captain that Sand Shan would not move in this weather. The guerrilla leader would be holed up, too. Yet Deacon hoped that Shan wasn't too far off. The going, even on a broad track, might soon become next to impossible. Streamlets would be transformed into raging torrents. The rivers would become impassable and slimy mud, washed off the base of the ridges, would clog the roadway. If Shan was more than four or five miles away, there was little chance that he would make the rendezvous by dawn.

Without doubt, the SAS teams backed across the state would also be in trouble if the rain continued for any length of time. Tim Dalinart, Pawson and Hornby would not be able to force a trek, to close off Shan's lines of retreat.

Under the folds of the cape, Deacon shivered.

After a couple of hours, the thunder rolled away to the east and the lightning died out. But rain continued to fall and the wind, though abating, was vigorous enough to toss the trees. Soaked through and chilled, there would be no sleep now for the soldiers.

Crawling, dog-like, on hands and knees, P.B. McNair approached the captain.

'Deke, we can't sit tight now.'

'Indeed we can't,' said Deacon. 'If Shan's in the vicinity, he'll come through to seek warmth and shelter at the mine. We've got to be certain when he makes his move.'

'What time is it?'

'Only about nine.'

'Christ! Nine or ten hours 'til the bloody sun comes up.'

'Let's get off this damned ridge. Rain or no rain, we can't afford to stay here.'

'Okay,' said the Scot. 'I'll shake Buz out.'

Laden and even wearier than before, the three men started down the steep side of the ridge. Steady, heavy rain provided a kind of faint illumination. Underfoot, conditions were treacherous. Groping like blind beggars, tapping with steel *parangs*, falling and grunting, torn by the thorns and spiked leaves, the soldiers inched downhill. Never had Malaya seemed so primitive and inhospitable – yet they were less than a mile from electric light and radio. It took until midnight to negotiate the ridge. Deacon could not be sure when they reached level ground. Water ran everywhere, a noisy flood that gushed through the undergrowth and rivered out on to the plain, while the rain hissed unrelentingly and the drowned jungle gurgled with rising freshets and springs.

The grassland gave Deacon his first real clue as to their position. Trees had thinned and shrubs diminished. The breast-high, broad-leaved grass was like a reed bed, only softer. He pushed through it, parting it with his forearms. His cape crackled and whispered as he thrust forward. When he stopped he could hear Buz and P.B. behind. But at least he knew where they were. They had reached the overgrown paddi which surrounded the east side of the track. He tried to make sense of shapes, to read contours, but it was impossible. The darkness was unrelieved by moonlight or stars, and the rain fell.

Ahead, though, was a pinprick of light; a window.

It gave Deacon perspective, dimension.

He waited until Buz bumped into him then drew the sergeant down. P.B., too, crouched on his knees in dabbling mud. Though the grass was over their heads it gave them no protection from the rain.

Covering his mouth with his hand, Deacon murmured, 'This is as far as we dare go tonight.'

'We could take the goddamned mine,' muttered Buz.

'It's far too much of a gamble.'

'Don't see how. We could wait for Shan – inside.'

'For God's sake, Buz! Do you want to risk blowing it, just for the sake of a dry bum?'

'Forget it,' Buz muttered. 'Yeah. You're right. We gotta wait here.'

'How long now?' said P. B. McNair.

'Half a dozen hours.'

'In this shit?'

'Do you have an alternative suggestion, Corporal?'

'Not me, sir.'

'Then kindly shut up.'

Colonel A. K. Saunders approached his finest hour with anxiety. On the surface you couldn't detect a trace of self-doubt, but the heavy rains had altered the situation and Saunders, like the troops in the paddi, had lost his faith in the elaborate plan of entrapment.

What worried him most was not 'his end' of the thing, but the weakness of the 'cork' that would plug the narrow funnel beneath the limestone ridge. Beyond was wild, dense jungle, and Shan was a jungle fighter. The little bastard, for all his Oxbridge appearance, could vanish into the great green like a tree-frog. The SAS might be supermen but they could not grow wings and fly. Saunders knew only too well what conditions would be like in the Tennga Valley and how swiftly tracks would be washed out and every rivulet transformed into a torrent.

It was too late to call the whole thing off. He had too many men in the field. At least communications between Shan and King would be cut off. The radio jammer had been a stroke of genius. The tropical storm would calm any suspicions that the guerrilla or the Fat Cat might have as to why the radios had ceased to function. Shan would expect King to be there; King would expect Shan.

All the Special Branch officers that Saunders could muster were 'on parade'. Plus a platoon of uniformed Malayan police, the pick of the bunch, marksmen all and all proven in action, standing 'on alert' in the yard of the old drill hall in Kuala

Lumpur's most northerly suburb, on the Sultan Mudhine boulevard. Three trucks were fuelled and ready to go. A telephone call from the landline that Saunders had had rigged from the junction of the North Road and the old Dejur highway would have the policemen tumbling out and the trucks in motion within minutes. A pair of agents, each with a portable short-wave radio set, were situated at strategic points on Lee King's route. The receiver in the back of the Bedford van was tuned in for the all-important message, *Lee King on his way.*

In a black Daimler staff-car, with insignia removed, Colonel Saunders, a senior driver and an armed police aide waited comfortably enough in a lane by an orchard behind the Assistant Health Inspector's bungalow. The lane was a mere five hundred yards from the turn of the North Road and the arch of palms which led into the Dejur highway. The radio van was parked directly behind the Daimler. A jeep containing four combat instructors was hidden by the fence which marked the end of the Health Inspector's garden.

Saunders peered out of the windscreen at the driving rain. It must be devilish uncomfortable in the jeep. Even with its top up and flaps down, it would be cold as charity. He hoped the instructors had had the sense to bring along extra woollens. How ridiculous, Saunders thought, to fret about the creature comforts of a quartet of men who were experts in suffering of one sort or another, laddies who probably slept on beds of nails and ate crocodiles on toast for breakfast.

Rain drummed on the Daimler's roof.

It was just plain cold now, like an English autumn. At least the electricity had gone out of the air. The short-waves would not be affected by static.

Saunders cleared his throat, causing the driver, who had been nodding over the wheel, to jerk and cry softly, '*Sah*?'

'Go back to sleep, Joseph.'

'Sah. I am sorry, sah.'

'Any more tea in that flask, Tom?'

'Plenty more, Colonel,' said the aide.

'Let's all have a cuppa, then, to keep us alert.'

Saunders' aide had just begun to pour tea from the Thermos when the lights of the Bedford van flicked on and off.

'Ah-hah!' said Saunders. 'Ah-hah!'

'Shall I go to see, sir?'

'Chop-chop, Tom. Chop-chop.'

The aide returned within three minutes. He could not suppress his excitement. He stood outside the Daimler's passenger door with a copy of the *Times* held over his head to keep off the rain, and beamed through the open window at the colonel.

'Come on, man. Out with it.'

'Lee King is on his way, sir.'

'Is there more?'

'He left his home half an hour ago and met the lorry at the railway station. It is the same as it has been before, Colonel. The Mercedes Benz motor car is to the front.'

'Is King in the truck?'

'King is in the truck.'

'Where are they now?'

'Heading this way.'

'Get in, Tom.'

It was early, much earlier than Saunders had anticipated. King, however, would not be oblivious to the weather conditions. He would be giving himself plenty of time to make it to Dejur by daybreak.

Calmly, Saunders sipped the lukewarm tea.

He did not, however, take his eyes off the rear-view mirror above the Daimler's windscreen. The next three-flash signal would indicate that King's truck had turned off the North Road on to the old highway. Saunders prayed that the agent on the telephone wouldn't panic and rouse the police detail too soon. Ten minutes was the time. Ten minutes after the quarry rolled into the trap before pursuit would begin. Saunders certainly didn't want to run into the back of Lee King's truck, or give the Chinese villain an indication that he was being followed.

It was a good hour until daylight. The Special Branch convoy would drive on low-beam. Headlights might be detected by King or his driver. Fortunately, the Dejur highway was tree-shrouded and anything but straight. But what if there was a delay? A landslip at the Timbakur Bridge? Flooding? What if the Mack should bog down? If that happened then Saunders would have no option but to pounce, take his chance that there was enough 'incriminating evidence' in the Mack truck to lead to a prosecution against Mr Lee King. It would be a farce, really, if all his planning went to cock because of a shower of rain.

'Lights, sah,' said the Malay driver.

Three flashes from the Bedford. Saunders had no need to send Tom back to unscramble the message. The signal was pre-arranged and specific.

'All right,' said Saunders. 'Take it slowly, Joseph. We're in no hurry. We're not chasing anybody, remember. Nice and easy.'

Joseph flicked the three-flash sign to the parked jeep before he drew the sleek Daimler out of the lane and prowled it, at no great rate, towards the North Road.

It was twenty minutes past four o'clock.

And still raining.

Pearled with raindrops, the stems of the guinea grass bowed. Deacon could hear the drip-drip-drip of water as the last breath of the night wind rippled across the *lalang* which bordered the grass patch in which he lay hidden. It was warmer now. A spectral mist wreathed the crest of the ridge and sifted down through the trees. In the sky there was a hint of dawn, of a sun which probably presaged a day of sticky humidity.

Deacon raised his head a little. The buildings of the mine were visible. All lights were out, though, and there were no signs of activity. It did not seem likely that, with so little to do by way of work, the employees would tumble out of bed early.

All around there was the din of flooding. The mine tailings showed water now, not lime-jelly mud. There had been considerable seepage over the sluices. On the inner slopes of the limestone, west of the pass, a thread of white water fell over a dark edge into the vegetation below. Bird sounds echoed from the trees. Soon, clouds of insects would hatch and add to the misery of the men in the paddi.

Shan was late. Deacon had expected that the CT leader would slink through the pass before full daylight. Perhaps he had been held up by the rain. More probably he had 'an approach' of his own, would not break cover until the Mercedes arrived. The SAS team was situated only fifty yards from the path across the paddi, not more than a hundred yards from the 'corner' of the ridge which protected the path. The scale of the landscape was miniature. Minus clinging jungle ferns, it wouldn't have made a decent training area. Sinking down again, Deacon glanced at his watch. Just after five-thirty. Shan was cutting it fine.

Grass roots still held water but it was draining fast now the rain had ceased. Buz Campbell had lain down, head supported on his pack, the shotgun valise held dry in his arms. His poncho was wrapped around his shoulders and head. His hips and legs were sodden. Mud caked his rubber boots, which tilted outwards at an odd angle. His features were worn, as if by the action of years of wind and water on porous rock, his beard speckled with silver. P.B. squatted by his buddy, wide awake, an unlit cigarette dangling from his lips.

P.B. raised an enquiring eyebrow.

Deacon scowled and shook his head.

'Shit!' said P.B., soundlessly.

At that moment, from the long grass to the left, a thin, singsong voice said, 'Do not move, please, gentlemen, or you will be killed.'

Deacon whipped round.

There were three of them, well spread. They all carried Browning submachine-guns. Even Sand Shan.

Unmistakable in an olive-green slicker and brown sou'-wester, the bill of which was pushed back from his brow, Shan's round, gold-rimmed glasses gave his eyes a terrible innocence.

Shan said, 'The soldier on the ground, instruct him to stand up, please.'

'Hey, Buz. We got company,' said P.B. McNair.

'Weapons down, and hands upward.'

The other CTs didn't look like dolts. If anything, they were more menacing than the boyish figure in the middle. Tall and muscular Chinese, in their early thirties, as near as you could tell.

Deacon thought: I could shoot him – and be shot. I could do it, kill him cleanly and be done with it.

'Better do as you're told, Buz,' said P.B. 'I'm no' very keen t' get blasted in the middle of a fuckin' paddi, this time in the mornin'.'

Slowly, Buz pushed himself upright. He glared redly at the communists.

'That him, Deke?'

'Absolutely.'

'You're a bastard, Shan, know that?'

'You are very stupid,' said Sand Shan, matter-of-factly. 'Now, tell me, where are the others?'

'Behind you,' said Deacon. 'Two platoons.'

Shan gave a smile that was less than skin-deep. 'There are no platoons behind me. I will give you the benefit of the question, Captain. I will believe that your comrades have been delayed by the rain.'

'Perhaps that's it,' said Deacon.

'Put the guns down,' said Shan. 'Immediately.'

With a gentle, casual motion, P.B. pushed the Enfield rifle from him into the grass. Deacon did the same thing with his Sten and, eyes fixed on Shan, unbuttoned his holster, hooked out his revolver and threw it, too, into the grass. Only Buz resisted. For a moment he was not quite rational.

'Shoot the sergeant,' said Shan.

'Wait, wait,' Deacon shouted. *'Do as he says, Buz, for God's sake!'*

Sand Shan laughed, shook his head at the futility of it all and, with a little wave of the hand, signalled Buz Campbell's execution.

The Browning to the left spurted flame.

Buz jerked, twisted and fell, one arm upraised, fingers hooked as if into a netting which would hold him upright. He fell on his back, twitched and rolled on to his belly. Shan did not come forward but put three shots into the grass where the sergeant writhed. Buz twitched, flopped and lay still.

P.B. yelled, *'Buz! Buz!'*

Deacon did not even glance at the body. He kept his icy blue eyes on Shan's face.

In a severe, peevish voice, he snapped out a command. 'Stand still, P.B. Stand absolutely still.'

'It is very commendable,' said Wei Sand Shan. 'Do you not see that I have men upon the hillside too? You cannot possibly escape me.'

'I'm surprised,' said Deacon thinly, 'that you came in person.'

'Do you regard me as a coward?'

'I thought you ran your shows from off-scene.'

'Off-scene?'

'May I attend my sergeant?'

'No,' said Shan.

'Bastard, fuckin' bastard!' Spit flew from P.B.'s lips.

'Come,' said Shan. 'It is time to get ourselves out of the open. We will go to the mine.'

Deacon said, 'How can you be sure the British aren't in possession of the mine?'

'An officer of your calibre is bound to be in the vanguard. If you had taken the mine, you would not have spent the night in the paddi.'

'Sand Shan, you don't recognise me, do you?'

'You are Deacon. Who falls from helicopters.'

'As a matter of curiosity, how did you survive?'

'I swam away.'

'Don't talk t' him, Deke. He killed old Buz. Christ, Deke!'

'Keep the head, P.B.,' said Deacon, still with that thinness in his tone, an air of cold, amiable logic. 'Say nothing.'

Shaking like a leaf, P.B. wept. He understood, though; his

grief was set apart from his hatred, from his belief that the Deacon would avenge the sergeant's death.

'Walk forward through the grass, please,' said Shan.

The CTs fell in around the SAS men.

Shan made a brief detour to look down upon the body of the Canadian. He seemed satisfied by his work. He nodded, stepped over Buz's legs and followed the group that had waded through the paddi.

Ten years of friendship lay behind Deacon and P.B. Buz had died without a whimper, without the chance to take an enemy to the grave with him in the last run-in.

From the lower slopes of the hill a dozen armed guerrillas appeared. Glancing round, Deacon realised that Shan had not lied.

Special Branch, and SAS veterans, should have known better than to weave rumour into fact. Sand Shan was excessively cautious and cunning. He did not, after all, travel without protection. Perhaps something had gone wrong with the radio messages and Shan had spotted the mistake. Would he have come at all, if that had been the case? To save Lee King, Fat Cat and supplier, agent for Peking? It was possible, even probable, that Shan's practical mind *would* work that way.

The whole damned thing was moot, really, Deacon decided.

A pale lemon sun was beginning to steam open the morning. Looking ahead, the captain saw that the workers at the Dejur mine had come out of the sheds. They were not, however, expecting the visit, or to see their comrades with SAS prisoners. Whatever could be deduced from the grim circumstances of the ambush, Deacon was now convinced that Shan did not know of Saunders' plan.

Glancing round once more, he noted that there were only a dozen in the CT unit. Shan hadn't left anyone on the high ground to act as scout. Deacon realised that he must take the blame for the fact that Shan had got the drop on them. Rain or not, he should have stuck to the ridge until daybreak. It had not occurred to him that the guerrilla leader would not simply come through the pass, that he would approach the mine with such exemplary caution, trekking his unit over the hill. An excusable under-estimation of the Red Number One had cost Buz his life and would, by the smell of it, cost them their lives too.

Long before the Security Force jeep could reach the mine, Shan would have worked out what was going on. What would the CTs do then? Make a run for it, like as not. King too? Come to think of it, King might even brazen it out. If there was no Sand Shan, no hard evidence, then King would not be on the rack. The Fat Cat would claim that he had simply made an inspection trip to his property, had no knowledge of 'bandit activity' in the area, had never met Sand Shan. Who would be around to deny the lie? Only P.B. and he knew of it, could stand in court as eye-witnesses. And P.B. and he would be dead.

The guards fanned out along the edge of the grassland. Shan had veered to Deacon's left, a safe fifteen yards away.

They were near the log-walk which surrounded the tailings.

Water bubbled unwholesomely in the rectangular ponds, the green scum stirred into a kind of froth. Deacon wondered how deep the ponds were. Deep enough to hold a couple of bodies?

Deacon's mouth was dry but he felt extraordinarily light-headed. It was almost like being tipsy on good French wine. Every sense, every impression seemed sharp. Shan's childish face, stuck with the glasses, and skinny neck reared above the green slicker. He had taken off the ridiculous sou'wester and slung it over his left arm like a posy basket. He did not look like a warrior. The gigantic Chinese rebel, Kwai Yan Chung, had seemed more suited to the role of leader.

'Are you going to shoot us, Shan?'

'I should have shot you many years ago, Captain Deacon.'

'Well, you did try.'

'That is true. Why are you here?'

'Routine patrol,' said Deacon.

'There have seldom been patrols in this area before now.'

The workers from the mine had armed themselves, Deacon noticed. They had carbines and a couple of submachine-guns.

But they were still unsure and kept their distance. No overseer or foreman came forward to speak with the guerrillas. It seemed as if that part of the story was true, that they did not know who Wei Sand Shan was and regarded him as a collector, a jungle courier.

Shan sidled closer to Deacon.

'If you do not tell me very quickly what you are doing here,' Shan said, 'I shall have your corporal shot, as I shot the sergeant.'

'Doing here?' said Deacon. 'What do you suppose I'm doing here? I'm looking for you.'

'How comical,' said Shan.

P.B.'s hands, clasped behind his head, parted. Deacon prayed to God that the Scot would not do anything rash. There would be time for courage later, if he could just delay Shan a little longer.

The high road to K.L. was visible. It lay straight for a half-mile or so across the plain before the vegetation crowded round it. From the north end of the mine workings, Deacon had an excellent view of the landscape, including the all-important section of open road. If there was to be deliverance, it would come up that road in the shape of Number One Copper.

'It isn't at all comical, Shan,' said Deacon. 'I'm perfectly serious.'

'It is a trap, is it not?'

'Of course,' said Deacon.

'And is the trap sprung yet?'

'It won't be sprung now.'

P.B. flexed his forearms and fixed his fingers together again. He angled his head so that he could see Deacon's expression. There was nothing to read there, only a familiar arrogance which indicated total indifference to disagreeable events. The Deke's white-blond hair clung lankly to his brow; he had lost his beret somewhere. His chin was tilted in refusal to submit to fear.

'Will you please tell me why that is?' said Shan.

'Because we had bad luck with the rain,' said Deacon, with a fleeting shrug of his shoulders. 'We British have never quite adjusted to this wild and woolly country of yours.'

'Do you know why I am here?'

'Haven't a clue,' said Deacon.

'You are lying, Captain Deacon.'

'Absolutely not, old chap.'

Oh, Christ, thought P.B. McNair, if Deke keeps on patronising the wee bastard, we'll be shot for sure, before we can do a bloody thing to warn the others.

But Jeff Deacon was taking a gamble on the fact that the guerrilla still needed them, that Shan, too, was unsure.

Deacon went on, 'Surely you expected us to be out and about, after that *contretemps* at the Port?'

'I do not understand what you say.'

'French,' said Deacon. 'After the *massacre.* Is that more comprehensible to you, Shan? *Massacre* is a word you surely understand?'

Now, how is this? thought P.B. With a dozen guns behind us and a dozen more in front, and thirty yards of open ground between us and the grass, what's Jeff playing at? He looked at the water at his feet and wondered how long he could stay under, and how deep the pond was. Despair crept over him. With Buz dead back there, there didn't seem much point in anything. Shan had fucked them again, good and bloody proper.

Far down the road a windscreen glinted in the pallid sunlight.

'Visitors,' said Deacon, affably, nodding. 'Expecting company, are you?'

The silver-grey Mercedes Benz was travelling fairly rapidly over the muddy surface of the road.

Sand Shan swivelled. He took a couple of steps towards the pond, to bring the curve of the road into view: an unguarded moment. Indecision had infected the guerrilla leader and transferred itself to the CTs and mine workers. They knew, of course, what the appearance of the Mercedes signified. But Shan was momentarily confused. Had it been in his mind that the whole thing was a set-up, that Lee King had sold him out to Saunders' Special Branch?

Deacon slanted his shoulder and peered behind him, back at the paddi.

In five minutes, ten at most, Saunders' coppers would crawl to a halt a half-mile down the high road. The timing was off. Beggars and dead men, however, can't be too fussy.

'Yes,' Deacon shouted. *'Now.'*

He flung himself headlong at the Scot and bore P.B. to the ground.

Dying, Buz realised, wasn't going to be so goddamned difficult after all. You spent twelve years training yourself to ignore pain and to get your body and will to work together when you ordered them to, and you couldn't even let yourself go when it came to the end of the line. He had no need to pretend any more. He wasn't faking it when he went ass-over-elbow into the paddi. He had two fat slugs in him and a welter of torn tissue and shattered bone above the left hip. A belly wound too, an exit hole, and a warm, saturated sensation below the waist.

Blacked out? Yeah! Maybe his brain had more savvy than he gave it credit for. The system had shut itself off. He didn't even remember the third bullet. Shan, the little yellow sonuvabitch, had missed. Nearly. The third slug had grooved his cheekbone and bored through the soft flesh of gum and cheek. Now his mouth was full of blood.

His head hummed like a spinning-top, like a toy he'd had when his old man came back from selling stock in Slocan one summer before they quit the farm. Hell, that tin spinning-top was near as tall as he was. He could clearly see its shapely wooden handle and metal corkscrew, and painted animals upon it – deer and bison and bears. His old man had gotten down on the cabin floor with him, smiling, and put the top on a smooth board, smiling, and had pumped the handle. And the top leapt upright, and the top sang. It was like the painted animals were singing, yeah, magically singing. His old man was laughing.

God Jesus! He hadn't thought of it in forty years, except when he was really sick one time and had dreamed of it and wakened and wondered if it had ever happened.

Maybe he would waken now, snap out of fevered sleep and find none of it had happened, that his whole life had been a dream. But the taste of blood flooding his mouth was too real, the gigantic humming in his skull too loud to be a dream.

Papa? I want my Papa. I want it all again. Please, Papa, let me go with you. Papa went out into the cold 'cause he was a big man and the cold didn't eat him up. Papa wasn't frightened of the cold and the huge white mountains. Let me go with you, Papa, please.

Buz Campbell opened one eye.

His face was pressed into watery mud among grass roots. His nose was crushed. He could not take air except through one nostril. One eye was under water. Warm, though, pressing like a membrane on the lid. Blood filled his cheek. He sagged his jaw to let it leak out. The water was a rusty red all round. On the ridge of the poncho, where it buckled under him, was a neat splash of red, like it had been done artistically with a brush, an elongated quotation mark, fresh on the rubberised surface.

The body, in shock, sent out no signals of pain. Only when Buz tried to stir his legs did his nerves tell him how bad it was down there. The humming in his head became so loud he could hear nothing else. Everything that the one good eye could see spun like the painted animals on the rim of the musical top.

Buz didn't feel good.

For all sorts of reasons, he felt lousy.

Hey, wee man? You there?

Say somethin', P.B. For Chrissake, speak to me.

Moving his lips caused a hot, wet flow to choke back into his throat. Buz quit at once. Pain was intense. Pain dragged him out of a comfortable ooze, a lovely long slide into oblivion. He just wanted to lay there, let it happen. But he couldn't.

The holes in the grass-matted mud were large. Two of them. Buz peered curiously into them, wondering what lived inside.

Snake, ant, beetle? Bullets. Bullets lived inside the two burrows. Goddamned close to his head. Four, five inches, buried into stiff Malayan earth. Friggin' bullets.

Buz began to fit together the correct sequence of events.

No doubt about it, he was a gonner. You didn't need no medical report to figure it out. Half of him was dead already, the other half on the chute. Right, wee man? Right, Buz. He wondered where P.B. had gotten to. And the Deke. He thought he could hear voices, the sigh of icy winds in tall mountains. Coldness shouted to him, like a cry. When he shifted his torso, the pain was so fierce he almost blacked out again. Holy Jesus, what was happening? With a massive effort, Buz cocked his right knee under his belly and operated his hip joint. He got himself two feet clear of the deck, saw the stalks of grasses, fluffy nodes on the top of the stems, the light of a thin morning sun dappled with the water droplets that hadn't steamed off the paddi. He stuck down his right arm and braced it, locking the elbow. He held himself there, neither lying nor kneeling, but somewhere in between.

The machine had gone *phut*. Will-power wasn't gonna do him any good now. He didn't even understand why he was trying so hard, since he could just as well stay where he was and wait for the tall mountains to come to him, for Papa to fling open the door and let the cold, crystal-clear brightness envelop him too.

If he hadn't felt so bad, so downright lousy, maybe he would have waited where he was.

He gathered blood in his mouth and spat. The effort racked him bad. He heard himself splutter. But he was thinking again, his skull spinning to a sudden stop, leaving no illusions and no dreams.

Buz Campbell groaned.

Sweat drenched him, sweat and rainwater and blood. He felt like a reptile. Funny, he always figured he would die in the desert. At night, under the clear, cold stars.

He worked the right hip and leg again, causing agony in the small of his back. It was like being hit with a shear-spike or the blade of a pickaxe. Slowly, he began to drag forward, right arm and right leg, steeling himself for the *whop* of pain with every movement. He didn't even think about his mouth now, though his face was hammering, hammering too.

It surprised him to find the valise with the shotgun in it, strapped around his left wrist.

Half a man. The left hand not belonging to him. But it worked. It was mechanically okay. Looking down the torn side of his body he saw the fingers of the left hand flex and wriggle in response to the message he had despatched from his brain. Hey, yeah! See that, wee man? Ain't it pretty! He waggled his fingers some more. He saw the strap which was stitched to the canvas valise slip. Felt it in his hand. He fished it towards him. He prodded and jerked at it until it came all the way up through the plopping blood which emerged from the front flap of the poncho. He got it in front of him, nudged it across the ground until it was close to his right hand too.

Now he had two hands to work with, something to concentrate on. He eased himself on to his right elbow, ignoring the pain. He picked and worked at the strap until he got it clear of the buckle. Left thumb and forefinger delicately flipped open the hood of the valise.

A hand-grenade rolled out.

Buz grinned with the right side of his face.

Cute, sitting there like a green egg in the watery slime, that British-made fragmentation grenade, a nice neat handful.

Buz shook the felt-padded valise and another green egg rolled out. Buz closed his fingers round it and bent his elbow. The old elbows and hands were functioning fine. Christ, man, he could thread a goddamned needle, right? He pushed the grenade into the top of the collar of the poncho and felt it slip ponderously into the pouch that his shirt made, crossed by a bandolier at the chest. There were no shells in the bandolier. He had left them dry and snug in the valise, along with the Vaughan shotgun.

Buz grasped the second grenade and pushed it into the shirt pouch too. It dismayed him to discover how the effort sapped his strength. His whole perspective was changed by the wound; he wasn't the man he had been just ten minutes ago, wasn't a man at all now. The feeling of dispossession was almost overwhelming.

Racing against time had become paramount, meant something more than just jigging along. He couldn't even think of Shan, of any objective beyond the simple actions – one at a time, Buz, you stupid sonuvabitch – that his hands had to do. It took an age to ease the cartridges from the strip pocket in the valise and spread them on the ground. Took less time, though, to unsheath the Vaughan.

Leaning his chest against the stock, Buz broke the barrel and held it open, the twin-bore muzzle held tightly under his armpit. He would have used his teeth but his mouth was mush. He had no sensation in it at all, and a crazy fear that he might swallow one of the brick-red shells. He got two into the breech of the Vaughan and closed it. There were too many shells on the ground. He couldn't cope with such a number. He managed four into the slots in the bandolier and two more in his right fist. He had been doubled over in that patch of the paddi for so goddamned long that the spot was puddled with blood. The mud under his knees was thick and crimson.

Hey, he thought, it's just as well I'm a big guy and got lots to lose. He put his nose against the stock of the shotgun, and watched sweat run down the polished wood like tears.

Seemed he had been manacled into the action for hours. But a grain of horse sense told him it couldn't have been all that long; three or four minutes, most like. Everything was winding down, distorted, like the music that came from one of the thick, black discs his sister had when she was young, and played on a crank gramophone. He tried to get back in tempo, to restore the beat. He was weakening, though, and it wasn't so easy. Still, the frag grenades were light. He could push them up Shan's ass if he could find some kind of cover in the *lalang*.

He hadn't been paying much attention to the landscape. He'd been drowsy and disgruntled in the rain-lashed half-light, before the CTs caught him. How many hundred yards was it to the mine? He angled the Vaughan in his elbow, set the barrel across the side of his neck, holding it as tight as he could with what was left of his jaw. The pain wasn't so much. Didn't go deep now, lay like a varnishing of caustic across the surfaces of his body. Jesus, though, he could feel it in the base of his spine, the grating of bone on bone. Maybe the bullets were still in there.

Okay, Sergeant Campbell, screw pain and self-pity. You gotta make it on the hoof, right? Time to shove off, buddy. Time to ride the tiger. The only discharge from this goddamned outfit was when they signed you dead. And you ain't dead yet, Sergeant Campbell.

Once he got mobile it wasn't so bad.

He pushed his head forward, rowed with his hands and let the wreckage drag after him. He got support and thrust from his right knee and foot. But the rest was meat, soft like hamburger. He tried not to think about it. He kept the blubber around his chops compressed to stop himself grunting. He wouldn't be kissing no girls for a long time. Susu would have to be patient. Patience had never been the kid's strong suit. He would explain to her, though, about loyalty and good faith. Susu would understand. Sure she would.

There was no horizon, except parting grasses. He was only a couple of feet off the deck, about the height of a fair-sized croc. He waddled, croc-like, through the watery paddi. But a soldier's sense of direction was still going for him. He reckoned he was coming close to the hem of the grassland, foot by foot, yard by yard. Blood dragged behind him like a snail's trail. What if the Chinks had dogs! Buz chuckled without sound, deep in his chest. Dogs? Jesus, Sergeant, you just gotta find something to worry about, ain't you?

Buz reached the thinning edge of the paddi none too soon. Everything was beginning to cloud, dim. He couldn't squeeze juice into his muscles much longer. He was cold too, very cold. The sky had iced over, all streaky white like a blizzard. He could hear the humming in his skull again, musical and magical, drawing him into it like a soft, soft vortex.

But he had come this far, enveloped in effort. Now he had to reconnect. Not for long, though. Just long enough to give the bastards hell. You come into the world yelling, you go out the same way. Right, wee man? Right, Sarge, right.

Buz rested on the shotgun stock. Carefully, he wiped his brow with the heel of his hand, stripping away sweat and mud from his eyes. Christ, but he was dry. He could have sunk a pint of the wee man's whisky, even the Deke's pissy gin. Lowering his head, Buz let the blood gout trail stickily to the ground. He closed his lips again. He rowed forward, three, four, five yards. Stopped. He propped his chest on the gun stock. He couldn't put it off any longer.

He raised himself up.

God must wear a dagger and stripes after all. God had steered him in a straight course through the paddi.

Buz was fifteen yards from the edge of the grass, thirty from the group by the edge of the tailing pond. He sucked breath through his nose. The humming had ceased. He was still cold but at least he was connected again.

The Deke and P.B. had their hands behind their heads. The position of submission and surrender didn't sit good with his old buddies. He would have to do something about that before he opened the door and strode out into the cold, bright light, after Papa.

He didn't bother to count the bandits. He was vaguely aware of their disposition. He couldn't even say which one was the leader, Shan. Sand Shan. One little thing at a time, Sergeant. But you better not tarry too long.

Hold it, just hold it.

God, he didn't even *care* which one was Sand Shan.

Fingers found the egg in the pouch by his breast. Warm, familiar. Automatically, he brought it towards his mouth, then halted the action. He held it, the grenade, in his left hand, flicked out the stiff pin with his right thumb. He didn't catch the spring and, with a surge of panic, reared and pitched the goddamned object outwards. He knew it wasn't going to make the distance. But he saw Deacon pivot, just a split second before the grenade rolled and scutted along the dirt. Deacon shouted.

Blood pumped from a gaping wound in Buz's gut. It astonished the sergeant. He felt an evacuation of his bowels and a release of urine, shocked by the sudden violent ebbing of vital force. He sat back, lifted the shotgun and, as the grenade exploded, triggered both shells simultaneously.

Scrambling, draining, Buz broke the breech and rammed the shells in his hand into the apertures. It was all one action now, one final, continuous motion. He snapped the shotgun shut and stood up.

Dirt whistled past him.

Hold it right there, Papa. I won't keep you long.

Out of the ice-cold, white-cold curtain there came light. It was brilliant and inviting. Marred only by the shapes of men, the enemy.

The two terrorists fired at the grotesquely bloodied figure which stood upright in the grassland, a Vaughan shotgun jammed firmly against its hip.

Buz held aim.

Papa? Okay?

Buz tugged the trigger cleanly one last time.

Saunders put his hand on Joseph's arm and said quietly, 'Brake down and stop, please.'

The Malay driver obeyed. The staff car slithered and came to a halt.

'What is it, Colonel?' asked Saunders' aide, his hand on the butt of his revolver.

'We're as good as there, don't you know.' Saunders twisted in the seat and peered back down the road. Its surface was scattered with puddles, drying now that the sun was up. Steamy ground mist clung to the light brown mud and fingered its way into the forest.

'One mile, sah?' said Joseph, the driver.

'Oh, less, less.' Saunders heaved a discreet sigh as he saw the canvas-topped jeep prowl around the bend. 'Ah, there are the laddies now.'

The jeep crawled to a halt fifteen yards behind the Daimler. Saunders waved and received acknowledgement with a flash of the vehicle's headlamps.

The Special Branch man was decidedly relieved to have reached the close proximity of the Dejur mine without mishap and without spooking Lee King. Already the colonel felt satisfied. His expression was smug as he unlatched the passenger door and thrust his shoulder against it. The door, like the rest of the car's bodywork, was armour plated. It took effort to open it. The colonel got out. Tom, the colonel's aide, climbed out too and the two men looked at each other across the roof of the motor car.

Jungle was all around; dense, second-grade forest, knitted with fern and creeper. The ochre slash of the road vanished into it twenty-five yards ahead of the Daimler. It was like being in a canyon. The forest was brim-full of sounds. Face smooth and innocent, the Malay Inspector listened with head cocked and brown eyes slanted. He had ears as sharp as a bat's and Saunders let him use them in peace for a moment.

Inspector Tom shook his head. 'I hear nothing, Colonel.'

'Well, we'll take a toddle, Tom.' Saunders held up his hand like a traffic policeman to indicate to the heavy mob in the jeep that they should wait where they were, then he led the Malay Inspector forward through the puddles.

Hugging the side of the road, above a rudimentary ditch which chuckled with rain-water, the two men took only a couple of minutes to round the curve. Through the elbow, they had an unimpeded view of the plain and, not far off, the Dejur tin mine.

The shaggy hummocks of the limestone ridge appeared to have been combed up by the storm and a sinister steam rose from the summits into the hazy lemon sky. Even without the use of the powerful field-glasses which Tom uncased and handed to his boss, Saunders could make out the Mack truck weaving the last quarter of a mile towards the camp. He could see nothing of the Mercedes Benz, however. Presumably it was blocked from his sight by the bulk of the American transporter.

Puffs of diesel smoke rose from the skinny pipe above the Mack's cab. The mine area appeared to be deserted.

The colonel raised the field-glasses.

At that moment a grenade exploded.

The spout of earth and smoke was tiny and frail at the distance. Even so, the colonel reared to his full height, flinching.

'God of my fathers!' he cried. 'Deacon's panicked.'

He flung the field-glasses back to the Inspector and, waving both arms furiously, urged the Daimler and the jeep to him. Spurting forward, the staff car skidded up beside the colonel. But the angular Englishman had gone haring past it, yelling to the assault team in the jeep. *'Follow me. Follow me in. Get the troops out and spread.'*

Behind the jeep, close together, were the three-ton trucks which contained the Special Branch hunters.

It had been Saunders' intention to disperse the detail and encircle the mine, fashion a cunning net which, like a purse, he would draw tight when he was sure that Shan and King were within. But that damned impetuous fool of an SAS man, Deacon, had ruined the plan at the last moment. Lee King would be out of the truck with his money bags and other 'incriminating evidence' and into the forest in a trice, and Shan would be darting away like a swamp rat, with all the space in the world to hide in. Damn Deacon. Damn the SAS.

Saunders stepped on to the running-board of the Daimler by the driver's door. Through the glass he could see Joseph's startled visage. Joseph started to fumble with the window, to lower it, but the colonel would have none of it. There wasn't a minute, not a blessed bloody second to lose now. He hammered his fist furiously on the car roof, bawling, *'Drive, you little devil, drive, drive, drive, I tell you, drive.'*

Collecting his wits, Inspector Tom grabbed hold of the handle of the passenger door and danced on to the adjacent running-board just as Joseph got the message and flung the car into gear. Squirting mud, the Daimler shot forward and slithered into a snaking swerve as the Malay fought to control it through the curve. He got the rakish nose straight in the nick of time and pulled the wheels into line, snapping the back end outwards and round, powering the car forward.

More stable, but with less power under its hood, the jeep negotiated the bend in the road and also debouched into the straight. Even with full acceleration it was unable to close the widening gap between the Daimler and the rest of the convoy. The drivers of the three-tonners, not anticipating this sort of rally-style charge, were caught between gears and lost even more ground. They came awkwardly out of the jungle on to the plain, by which time Joseph's foot was slammed to the floor and the staff car was rocketing along the straight, eating up the ground between it and the bulky, black-painted diesel truck.

Saunders clung to the running-board for dear life. He was mad with frustration and excitement. The wind whipped his hair about his cheeks and mud sprayed his lower body, bathing his neatly-pressed trousers in a deluge of brown. So rapid was the approach that he could hardly breath, yet he found the lung power to shout continually, bawling like an old chieftain on his war-horse. Inspector Tom, the colonel's aide, pressed himself close to the panel, keeping as bunched-up as possible, hanging desperately on to the door handle and the rim of the windscreen.

Half-blinded by wind-tears, the colonel could not discern just what was happening up ahead. Certainly it was no all-out attack. There had been only that one explosion and he did not catch the bark of the shotgun or the rattle of responsive fire and saw nothing, of course, of Campbell in the paddi or of Deacon. But the colonel, in the reckless days of his youth, had been a Flying Squad officer and had ridden fast cars through the streets of London. He knew all about raiding and pouncing, and, with dangerously wild gestures, urged the driver on, on into the heart of the Dejur and right up the arse of that big, black, smoke-spewing, American truck.

'Drive,' Saunders bellowed. *'Drive, you 'orrible coolie. Drive, drive, drive.'*

Softly, softly would catchee no monkey now.
It was time for the clenched fist and the big stick.

Deacon knew that this would be the end of it, the end of everything, that it would happen quickly now. The entire SAS ethos balled into response. All his years as an officer gathered in him, giving him the kind of strength that the Crusaders of old had had, a conviction of truth and the rightness of his actions. That last fleeting glimpse of Buz stamped itself into Deacon's heart and brain; the burly bear-like Canadian dragging himself through the paddi, shattered by bullets, to end with a gesture of courage and defiance which few would ever know about.

The grenade came out of the grass like a cricket ball bobbing towards the long boundary. This, Deacon realised, was his one chance, his only chance. When he dived on P.B., the grenade had already exploded. Covering the corporal, head down, Deacon protected himself as best he could from whistling shrapnel and flung dirt. But he was up and on his knees before Buz Campbell pulled the trigger of the Vaughan.

The CT nearest Deacon collected the grenade blast full on and was blown three or four feet backwards, pitted with metal fragments. His gun, a Browning submachine-gun, skidded flatly from him as he swept up his arms to protect his eyes. A second CT was caught by the spray from the shotgun shell. He bounced backwards too, tripping and pitching into the pond. Shoving P.B. with his knee, Deacon dived backwards and neck-rolled as somebody – Shan perhaps – let off shots at him.

The shotgun boomed again, though Buz was no longer visible above the level of the grass. Bandits plunged through the *lalang* towards the spot. Mine-workers scattered in search of shelter. Deacon grabbed the Browning on the run and changed direction sharply as a swarm of bullets dusted the earth close to his legs. Crouched, the weapon in his left hand, he sprinted towards the ditch which bordered the end of the high road, then whirled and, kneeling, fired.

He had fewer targets than he had anticipated. A few armed

CTs were dispersing – regrouping? – on the far side of the ponds. Several had dashed into the paddi. Obviously they thought that an SAS squadron had popped out of the bush, not just one man, a man who should have been dead. Deacon fired with lethal accuracy. He killed two guards outright before they could pick up on him, winged three others. In the paddi, four more bandits pranced outlandishly away from him.

Deacon glanced to his left, searching for P.B. The little Scot had lost none of his speed. He was already tail-down in the drainage ditch, scuttling along it towards the pass, the mouth of the Tennga.

Deacon knew better than to suppose that P.B. was retreating from the fight. The Scot was narrowing the angle on the paddi. In the paddi were abandoned guns and P.B. needed a weapon. Out of the paddi he could fight and fight well, better than any damned guerrilla.

Deacon turned, ran and dived into the broad ditch. It was almost full of flowing water. He hoisted the Browning high to keep it from getting wet as he slid his body down into the water, almost to the chest. He glanced to his left again. P.B. had disappeared into the paddi. Deacon dropped the sub-machine-gun into position, braced on the rim of the ditch. He tilted it and fired again, a short, economical burst, and downed one of the bandits who had rounded on him.

Where the devil was Shan, though?

When he darted his eyes to his right, Deacon was amazed to see a Mercedes bearing down on him. He swung from the waist and crooked the metal grip of the Browning into his elbow. He balanced the muzzle and stood up suddenly, firing. The Mercedes' windscreen starred and streaked, smeared into opacity. He fired again, got the tyres. Slewing, the Mercedes ploughed on. It rammed into the sluice stanchions, ripping them down. Boards slanted and clattered. A torrent of gravel-water vomited on to the track. By that time, Deacon had put another burst, broadside, into the Mercedes. He had the satisfaction of seeing the heavy vehicle nose-dive into the tailing ponds.

Behind the Mercedes was Lee King's truck; much larger than Deacon had thought it would be. It was a piece of ponderous transport, snorting black smoke. Its cabin screen, blanked out by light, looked like a slab of marble. Behind the Mack, though, was Saunders' Daimler. Deacon held fire, wasting no ammo on the huge truck as, slowing, its onside door flapped open.

Deacon ducked. Like a heavy bomber coming in to land on a country strip, the diesel truck had no room to manoeuvre. It could not avoid the inch-deep lake of gravel-water which had spewed from the buckled sluices. It hit the slipping mud on the brake and slanted into a magnificent pirouette, clumsy and ponderous, which carried it back-end first into a timber pile. Jagged showers of unstripped logs lanced in all directions. Mine-workers who had hidden there were flushed out. Two or more were crushed by the irresistible force of the American freight truck as it glanced off the pile and caromed into the gable of the end shed and vanished through it.

It was not the eventual fate of the Mack that concerned Jeff Deacon right there and then. He had spotted the figure of the plump, well-dressed Chinese. A shiny morocco-leather attaché-case was in his hand. He had leapt from the truck's flapping door and, dazed by the fall, knelt on all-fours in the middle of the roadway. No prize for guessing that the fugitive was Lee King, the Communists' paymaster, K.L.'s own Fat Cat. Deacon might have risked going out for him, but he had no opportunity to do so.

Even before the Mack bulled into the timber pile, a hundred yards away, Deacon's attention was caught by the speeding Daimler. Two men clung to the running-boards. One was instantly recognisable as Colonel Saunders. The gaunt, angular copper had pitched himself into action without regard for safety, let alone the dignity of his exalted office.

Everything had been compressed, bottled into one continuous incident, rich and heady. The capture of Lee King completed it. From the moment that Deacon had swung away from the paddi, from the appearance of the tumbling hand-grenade, only three minutes had elapsed. Buz was dead, of that there was no doubt. Saunders had not as yet worked his troops into the area in any strength of numbers. And Lee King, armed with a .38 automatic, was out and running.

No, Deacon realised, not running.

The Chinese reeled and swayed. He fired the .38 automatic at the Daimler. Deacon saw that Saunders was hit. His arm and shoulder flung backwards. One leg waved. Then the Daimler's front wing clipped Lee King, and Saunders heaved himself bodily and without thought of injury on top of the plump Chinese.

The .38 went off twice. All Deacon could see was Saunders' flailing arm and Lee King's kicking legs. The gun sounded a third time. The Daimler squealed to a halt, front tyres hard against the piling of the pond. Sensibly, the Malay aide had yanked open the car door and dived inside. The staff car was the target for sporadic rifle and submachine-gun fire from miners and guerrillas who had backed into positions across the ponds or in the edge of the paddi.

The .38 roared for a fourth and final time. Both men were still. Saunders slumped across the body of the Fat Cat.

'Saunders?' Deacon shouted. 'Colonel?'

It was comical, or would have been, under other circumstances, how Colonel Augustus Saunders sprang to his feet. He had been shot in the left arm and the fin dangled uselessly, like that of a marionette with a snapped string. But the rest of him was animate enough and he leapt and pranced over the body of Lee King and, in a sudden wild fit, kicked the dead man's buttocks.

'He's dead. Damn and blast him. Don't you know, he's dead.'

There was no more to be done. From the rear passenger door of the Daimler, the Malay aide emerged and, gun in hand, ran low towards the colonel. In addition, the police jeep was disgorging its crew and the three three-tonners had hove into position a couple of hundred yards away.

Any guerrilla in the Dejur area who wanted to evade arrest would have to fight his way out. Terrorists were breaking for cover, hastening through the paddi towards the narrow forest track which passed through the limestone hummocks into the Tennga Valley.

Holding the submachine-gun over his head, Deacon waded left along the ditch to cut off the most obvious line of retreat and, if possible, to locate and destroy Sand Shan.

P.B. McNair squatted in the *lalang*. Being a small man, the reed-like grasses at the border of the paddi patch came well above his head. Between his knees was the weapon he had retrieved by his dash into and through the grass; a treasure trove – the Enfield rifle. He still had a pocketful of bullets for it. The guerrillas hadn't had the savvy to search him. Somewhere over there, closer to the mine, was what was left of Buz Campbell, which probably wasn't much, come to think of it, since Buz had been cut down by a hail of bullets. P.B. couldn't quite grasp the fact that Buz was a gonner. The big sergeant had seemed, somehow, indestructible.

P.B. had lost a wheen of companions and comrades-in-arms over the years, but he had never been close to any of them, the way he had been to Buz and the Deke. Normandy, Russia, North Africa, Sicily – the march of the dead went back near a dozen years. After a while, it had seemed to him that he lived a charmed life, that he and Buz and Jeff Deacon were possessed of some odd aura that kept them, and would keep them, safe for ever. What a load of ballocks! You signed for a soldier and you sold your right to a future, like taking a ticket in a lottery, like riding the bloody tiger.

P.B. picked up the Enfield. He checked the ten-shot magazine. He could have done with a couple of grenades too, but he hadn't stumbled across any of those and counted himself fortunate to have found his own gun. With no time to hang about, he abandoned the position and ducked through the grasses, trailing the rifle in his left hand.

Last he had seen of the Deke, the captain was snug in the water-ditch by the end of the roadway. P.B. didn't try to guess what the Deke would do; wait for the arrival of the coppers from K.L., maybe. It didn't much matter. No 'plan' was possible. Christ, they were lucky to be operating at all. Thank old Buz for that, for buying them an opportunity to go down fighting.

Sun was up. Nice enough day. Visibility could have been better. Still an' all, he wasn't intending any long-range work. Fifteen hundred yards, that sort of thing. He doubted if he had the eye for it these days. Doubted if there was such a thing, fifteen hundred yards' clear shooting on the whole fuckin' Peninsula. It wasn't great country for a shit-hot sniper. In the end, you come down to what you are, clinging to what you do best. Like Buz. Like Buz hauling himself through the paddi with the blunt, comfortable Vaughan in his mitts. Buz had always been strong, like a bloody bear. Big bear. P.B. had always been nippy, a wee fox. He didn't know what the Deke was, except smart.

The corporal reached the scrumble at the foot of the ridge. He was no more than a hundred yards from the spot they had come down last night. Last night? God, it seemed like an eternity since they had stumbled out of the forest in the lashing rain, frozen and miserable, and waded out into the paddi patch. P.B. wasn't cold now. He wasn't even weary. The sprint through the grass had shaken him up. His blood was fizzing like cream soda in a bottle. He dabbed sweat from his forehead. Took two breaths and eased the Enfield lightly into both hands.

P.B. McNair lifted his nose above the grass. He had the hill behind him, rearing up, and a wide angle on the plain. The targets were spread. He could see a couple way off to his left, three, four hundred yards away, two guys plunging and bucking through the dry stuff in a bee-line for the thin edge of the forest.

He adopted a kneeling stance, perfectly steady.

Wetness seeped through the knee of his trousers, a cool penny-patch on his flesh. A faint drift of breeze, not enough to spin the bullets off, just enough to dizzy the insects that hovered above the paddi field. Bucking and plunging, thinking they'd got away, had a fuckin' future.

Wrong again, pals.

Two shots, fired almost simultaneously.

The bandits fell. There was no sound, except the faintest of squeals, like a stuck piglet.

P.B. dropped into the grass and tracked to his left.

He moved back on to the soft humus that flourished in places at the base of the hill, where the water caught. He was still in the shelter of the sea of grass, though.

He paused, rose, sighted.

Singles. Two CTs. They were separated by a dozen yards, had a hole of sorts on the right edge of the patch. Protecting the run to the pass? What'd it matter!

P.B. took a little more time since the targets weren't moving. He put them down, at four hundred yards or thereabouts, quick as winky.

A crashing noise behind him caused the corporal to whirl suddenly. But he did not lose balance, not for a moment. The Chink was high above and not quite ready to flay him with the submachine-gun – which was just as bloody well since P.B. hadn't counted on there being anybody behind him who wasn't retreating at a high rate of knots.

Ferns and spiky plants partly blocked the sighting but the bullet wouldn't be deflected by the young green stuff. P.B. took a couple of seconds to line the shot before he pulled the trigger. The commie was frantic, trying to get some kind of drop on him. Even when the Jap-made woodpecker spurted out a burst, P.B. didn't flinch. Breath sifted through his lips. Empty and steady, he fired twice. Bingo!

Kill number five.

P.B. lowered the rifle and trailed it, travelling laterally now around the base of the prow of the ridge, close to the mouth of the pass. He was conscious of the noises of attack from the mine and paused once to raise himself up.

Police wagons were in position. Sweeping lines of uniformed Malays were chasing across open ground to the south and east of the workings. On the roadway there was a long black motor car, nosed into the ponds, a Mercedes. He couldn't see the

Deke just at that moment, then snapped up the Enfield as Jeff moved into view in the ditch. P.B. had sense enough not to call attention to either of them by shouting. For all he could tell, the paddi was still littered with live bandits, awaiting an opportunity to head for the jungle, like rats from a harvest field.

He could guess where Deacon was headed, though. Into the mouth of the pass. It would be fifteen, twenty minutes before the coppers mopped up the mine area and got the net tight around the open ground. The Tennga offered the only real hope of escape for the guerrillas that were left alive. And that included Shan. And where Shan was, Deacon would be hot on the trail.

P.B. glanced up.

Tangled buttress just above him. Luxuriant plants spilled from four great trees and above that, lording it over the lower slopes, what looked like an oak, solid and familiar among the tropical growths. If he could get himself a post up there, with a view-line down into the Tennga, no saying what he couldn't find and kill. Every damned bloody commie bastard who thought he'd made it, driven before the regulated advance of the police troops, would have another think coming.

P.B. turned again. Deacon had disappeared. He had no way now of communicating his intention. Still an' all, the idea was bright. He was no jungle-rat; he was a sniper, best in the business, according to old Buz Campbell.

'Aye,' said P.B. softly and, crouched, headed up the hill towards the towering oak.

Leaving the action at the mine in Saunders' capable hands, Deacon climbed from the ditch and headed at a run for the mouth of the track. Sodden with water his clothing clung to him like a second skin. To his right, not far off, P.B. was working the paddi, cutting down the bandits who tried to weave through the grassland back into the Tennga. If Shan had gone to ground in the paddi patch he was cooked for sure. Saunders' crack troops were already spreading around the east flank of the mine area and, in a few minutes, would have swept a sickle of guns as far as the base of the ridge.

Deacon did not believe that Shan had taken cover. He felt sure that the CT leader had quit the Dejur immediately and had gained himself a head start.

From the ditch, however, Deacon had an extensive view of the shaggy slopes of the ridge and was willing to wager that Shan had not aimed for the lofty jungle trees but had navigated for the pass. What was more, if his rudimentary arithmetic was correct Shan was alone. It was possible that the Red leader had stashed a back-up unit in the valley, but Deacon was willing to take that chance. In fact he was willing to take any chance to trap the barbarous little fanatic.

The pipestem waterfall had almost dried up in the heat. It fanned a faint rainbow haze over glistening foliage. Shadows slanted from the ridge's western slopes, for the sun had gathered strength as it hitched itself over the treetops. After the storm the forest was lusher than ever, aromatic, and pulsating with the drone of insects, including a float of locusts which had been attracted by straddles of wild maize and leaf shoots.

Shagging the Browning in both hands, ready for firing, Deacon loped swiftly into the pass. He had no other weapon, and the mag was probably half-empty. But one round would be enough. He'd been saving one round, metaphorically, for Shan ever since that fateful night in '45 when Shan had shot three British officers in the back and had betrayed Deacon to the Japanese. Deacon wasn't thinking of pure revenge, though; he remembered, rather, all the atrocities he had witnessed since coming to Malaya, the wanton killings which branded Sand Shan as a man without compassion or a shred of mercy.

The rearing shoulders of the limestone closed about Deacon. He was a solitary soldier in congealing forest. Travelling fast along the clay-streaked path he soon detected the spoor – heel prints, skids and wedge depressions. Just the kind of tracks that a running man would leave in the aftermath of heavy rain. Deacon grunted and pushed on, following the signs. He had no difficulty with the spoor. One did not have to be a Dyak born in the jungle to read such obvious tells. A single runner in rubber boots had passed this way recently. The boots had a ridged sole, and the feet within were as small as a boy's. Sand Shan was the fugitive.

The Tennga opened a little to the sky beyond the flanks of the limestone hummocks. Trees were less tall and more densely packed. The undergrowth was matted like wire. Steaming humidity muffled all sounds, except the dynamo of the insects and the *churr* of the locusts. The air tasted sticky and sweet, like a sickly nougatine. Deacon ran with his gaze fixed on the dash-and-depression spoor, as it spooled out before him.

And then it ceased.

The ridges had not quite fallen behind the captain. Fifty or sixty yards ahead a scabrous, ragged palm tree had been washed out by its roots and had tumbled on to the path. Beyond it the path vanished. Elephant track or not, the forest consumed it like a strand of brown spaghetti.

Treading like a man on thin ice Deacon walked softly forward, peering. He darted his glance to right and left, continued another ten paces. No spoor. No tell-tale signs. Nothing. Shan had quit the path at this point. Shan wasn't going to run for ever. Shan hadn't given up and fled into the bush. No, Deacon could feel the guerrilla's presence in his water. Shan wanted him now just as much as he wanted Shan. That was all Deacon needed to know. Completion of equation.

With the Browning at the ready, cradled at waist height, Deacon stood up straight.

'Shan.'

The locusts roared and whirred. A minute blue bird with a throat full of rusty nails winged noisily across the pathway behind him.

Deacon swung round.

'Shan.'

The forest deadened echo. His challenge was smothered by the luxuriant growth. He swung again from the hips, glancing around, then fixing his gaze on the fallen palm tree.

'Shan,' he shouted at the pitch of his voice. *'Why don't you take the chance? Why don't you shoot me?'*

There was only a fraction of a second's warning, the slightest movement, the quiver of the hanging fronds of the toppled palm. Momentary stillness, chillingly complete, enveloped the valley, as if the locusts and black flies had hushed in expectation of blood.

Deacon dropped where he stood.

The submachine-gun squirted by the side of the quivering leaf, gas hot in the muzzle mouth. A stream of bullets teased the grasses half a yard from Deacon's head. He dived and neck-rolled into the pathside growth as Shan unsystematically strafed the verge. Bunched ferns, a mass of bright green fists unfolding in the day's heat, were chopped up and scattered over the SAS captain as he slapped belly-down. Instantly, without pause, he snaked forward, the Browning pushed ahead of him.

It was perfect.

Ah, Shan, you bastard, Deacon thought. Now I have you. You have shown yourself. You can't revert to your dirty, skulking cowardly terrorist tactics now. I'm no damned innocent, no poor native child with trusting brown eyes. I'm that which you will never be, Wei Sand Shan – a soldier.

Ah, yes, I have you where I want you, and I'm not going to let go.

Gauging the angle, Deacon bored left a dozen yards into the tilt of the bank that flanked the path, into the breast-high vegetation that boiled from the big tree roots. He ran hard, bent double, the Browning at knee height, and nothing to mark him except an occasional nod of fern in his wake.

There was no means of guessing precisely what Shan would do. He might retreat, might find another foxhole to snipe again. He might elect to hold the position by the toppled palm thinking that Deacon would not dare advance under fire, that he, Shan, still had the better position. Deacon was ninety per cent certain that Shan only had a Browning, an identical model to the one he had hoisted from the CT guard.

It was so terribly neat. Neat. Neat. Neat.

Deacon came to a halt, kneeling in the foliage. Breathing through his nostrils he made no sound at all.

What you don't know, Shan, is that I'm going to attempt the impossible, well, the highly impractical. You see, Shan, I'm damned-well going to take you alive.

Absolutely.

I'm going to take you alive to prove that it's possible to fight a dirty war and still retain some honour. To be an officer, a leader of men in the hardest outfit in any man's army, the SAS, and not fall foul of becoming a butcher too.

Make no mistake, I would love to kill you, to put a bullet through your head in memory of all the innocent people you've slaughtered and the carrion stink with which you've polluted this country. But I'm not going to be like you. I'm not your equal, Shan. I'm your superior, and I'm going to prove it to you. By taking you in unscathed.

'Shan.'

Deacon wriggled forward. He lay with the slope, head down towards the path. It was the best protective position a soldier could find. In the undergrowth there was small chance of Shan straying on the angle, finding him out with Browning fire. Deacon wormed down towards the path while, along the knuckle of the slope close to the trees, Shan's bullets mowed down the harmless plants.

A prolonged burst. A nice long wasteful burst. You damned fool.

Yes, Wei Sand Shan was afraid.

There would be nothing on that unseamed face or in the button eyes to tell you. But the freeze of the finger on the trigger of the submachine-gun was a sure sign.

Deacon grinned and bellied himself down to the very edge of the elephant track. Shan was struggling on the horns of dilemma. What should he do? Fight or retreat? Shan's confidence would be ebbing rapidly. Any moment now he might choose to make a break for it.

If I don't get too cocky, Deacon assured himself, I've got the swine where I want him.

The captain squatted on his haunches and frog-walked carefully through the spray of grasses of the inner verge. Without stretching he could have touched the path with the gun. But he was patient now, almost relaxed. Shan wouldn't know whether his shots had found target or not, and that would add to his uncertainty. Fifteen yards would bring Deacon to the fallen tree. He settled on his heels, the Browning across his knees. The strident acrimonious sizzle of forest insects enveloped him. Even so he could hear blood pumping in his heart.

In three or four minutes he would have Shan. Or he would be dead. In this game there was no half measure. In three or four minutes he would charge the hide.

But Deacon had underestimated Wei Sand Shan.

Out of ammunition but determined to be rid of the leech-like SAS officer, Shan had not clung uncertainly to the shelter of the palm. He had used the lull to go high, to better his position.

At that instant Shan sighted Deacon below him, to the left. He gripped the gun like a baseball bat. Weapon enough. Bareheaded, he had shed the proofed garment in the paddi. He wore a bush shirt without insignia, and duck pants. His thin features were not so youthful and his eyes were round and frightened behind the lenses of his gold-rimmed glasses.

Shan knew only too well that he would have only one chance. If he did not kill Deacon with the first blow, it would be all up with him. Planting his feet firmly in the soft ground, he flexed his legs, twisted his shoulders and loaded his weight behind the club-like weapon.

Swinging with all his might, he leapt down on Deacon.

Deacon caught the swish of the Browning as it made its deadly stroke. He flinched. Enough. The butt crunched into his left shoulder, fracturing bone. Fire raced down his arm, across the nape of his neck into his skull. Instinctively he sagged on to the path, thrusting the gun before him in his right hand. He tried to writhe round, tried to cant the muzzle round, to find aim. He tugged the trigger far too soon. Shots winged harmlessly into the bush. Shan drew back and swung a second time. The butt of the submachine-gun buried itself in the mud an inch from Deacon's belly.

Locking the gun under his armpit, Deacon half-rose and as

Shan made his third swipe, he drove the muzzle like a bayonet into the guerrilla's groin.

Shan cried out, gagged, and doubled over.

Like a wrestler springing from live canvas, Deacon surged upon him. The Chinese was no match for Deacon. Too light in weight and inexperienced in fighting he was powered at once to the ground. Ignoring the fractured shoulder, Deacon straddled Shan's chest and closed his fingers around the terrorist's wand-slender neck, his thumbs pressed deep into the gullet. Flailing desperately, Shan tried to shake the man loose. Remorselessly Deacon bore down, white-blond hair hanging, dripping sweat into his victim's face. Breath sawed in Shan's windpipe and in two or three minutes he would suffocate, unless Deacon's thumbs cracked bone first. Deacon was possessed by hatred, contorted by it.

A wheezing cry ripped out of Shan.

Deacon's features flared in surprise and he jerked back, sat bolt upright then, with the back of his right hand, delivered four smacking blows, and stood up.

'On your feet, Shan.'

The CT leader seemed incapable of movement. Fingers cupped his throat, he gasped and gagged, groaning, and when Deacon stirred him with his foot, rolled on to his side.

'Up. You heard me. Up. Before I change my mind.'

It would have been so easy to kill the guerrilla, to exorcise all the demons that tormented him, but Deacon did not believe in the efficacy of sacrifice. It lay outwith the code he had been raised to believe in.

'Get up, damn you, Shan.'

Bleeding from swollen lips, coughing, the bandit struggled to his knees and Deacon dragged him to his feet. His glasses dangled from his ear. Peering, fumbling and vulnerable he groped for them and fitted them upon his nose. He squinted at Deacon. There was pain in his body and he wasn't used to it, but it was quite superficial and there was no real wound, no injury.

'Kill me, Deacon,' Shan croaked.

Deacon shook his head. 'Oh, no, Shan. No, no, no! But I will be there at your trial, and at your execution. Whenever and wherever it takes place, I will be there.'

'Kill me.'

'Move.'

Deacon lifted the Browning from the grass and tucked it under his functioning arm, letting it ride in the crook of his elbow.

'If you run, Shan, I'll wound you. But I won't kill you.'

'Please, do it.'

There was a note of hopelessness in Shan's voice. He knew now that nothing he could say or do would cause his death at the hands of the SAS officer. The most he could expect would be a bullet in the calf of the leg. He wanted no more pain. What he craved was oblivion, a release from the future, from whatever shame would accrue to him with defeat. He regretted nothing, of course, only his capture and the hot human impulse which had impelled him to turn on Deacon, to fight like a man.

Deacon dropped back a yard. 'Walk.' He gestured with the Browning. 'Walk, Shan – and bear in mind that I'm behind you.'

Head hanging the communist leader turned towards the pass that would lead him to the Dejur, into handcuffs and a police cell.

The bough was warm between P.B McNair's thighs. He had a strong, comfortable grip upon it, ankles crossed. His shoulders were supported by the oak trunk. He had dried his face carefully with a handkerchief from his pocket, had wiped the stock of the Enfield and most of its metal parts, rimming the trigger guard and, with a loving touch, the trigger itself.

Clean and dry the rifle waited, laid across one thigh.

Nothing bothered the little Scot, not even the insects, the low champing *churr* the locust float made as it rose and shifted and latched on to the wild maize and baby leaves.

The corporal pinched a cigarette between finger and thumb. The paper was a bit damp and burned badly but the tobacco tasted great. The drag settled his nerves. He had command of the Tennga head and the mouth of the pass north of the plain. He had chosen the location in preference to the tree's sunnier side because he knew that the Deke had gone through, and Shan ahead of him. He had glimpsed the guerrilla leader, a strange skinny wee bugger, as he had darted from the path and on to the verge and had holed up in the leaves of the fallen palm up the road a piece.

How far up the road? Distance?

Five hundred yards.

P.B. had shinned up the oak with the rifle slung round his shoulder, had swarmed round the trunk from the blind side and had soon discovered this perfect position. He even had leaves to give screen, though not protection. Who the hell needed protection? From this stance P.B. watched Deacon's play.

Seemed bloody daft for a wee while, until he twigged the Deke's intention, and the reason for it. P.B. pursed his lips. The Deke intended to take the Chink alive, and he was pulling the old stunt to do it, advancing when the enemy expected him to be under cover, giving the gunner fun to draw his fire and squander ammo.

Pretty good, Jeff. But, Christ, wouldn't you be relieved to learn you've got me up here for back-up?

P.B. did not flick away his cigarette and prepare to shoot until Shan had left the hide and was on the hillside, weighing the Browning like it was a bat or a club. P.B. laid the rifle against his cheek just as Shan pushed the assault on Deacon, catching the officer by surprise.

Corporal McNair studied the struggle critically but without undue concern. It was the usual falling-about scrap, comical if you weren't involved. He knew the Deke would come out the winner.

P.B. eased his right arm and flexed the fingers. He leaned his shoulders against the tree but kept an easy eye on the fray. There was a bullet up the spout and the catch was free. He could plug Sand Shan any old time. But it wasn't his fight, his play – yet.

Contentedly P.B. breathed the scented air. A beastie coiled and uncoiled along the tip of the branch on which he sat. A centipede. You'd never see anything like that in Euston Station waiting room. Nothing like Shan either – not for the time being.

Come to think of it there were precious few left like Jeffrey Alexander Deacon, true-blue gentlemen. No room for them in wars like this one, in wars to come, maybe. Thank Christ he wasn't tarred with the noble brush. He was nothing but a fuckin' dog-soldier and carried no obligation to honour in the old-fashioned manner.

It wasn't for Buz that the Corporal licked the ball of his thumb. Buz had been a soldier and had died like a soldier. P.B. set his thumb very lightly across the base of the trigger guard. Who was it for, then? Susu Mafan, the wee whore who hadn't tasted enough of life to pick sides for herself? Aye, she'd do for a cause. The dead bairns in the abo village too, and the nurses in St Andrew's Hospital, and the planters' wives and daughters carved and burned for the sake of spreading the word about Communism. They'd all do, all the victims of the tyranny of expediency and principle that was creeping across the world, and was touted as the ultimate human right. Well, he was just a dog-soldier but he had his rights too, and his priorities. They included the right to judge by experience, to execute out of certainty plus a wee bit of low-grade selfishness that few folk would grudge him in that primitive, beautiful country on the far side of the world.

They were coming towards him now, Shan and Deacon.

The Deke was hanging cautiously back.

Shan's head was bowed. He looked sheepish, childlike, as if he had been caught doing mischief and not evil.

Aye, that was it. Evil.

Excuse it how you liked, tart it up with fancy names, the terrorists' trade was evil. And when you confront it, you no longer have doubts.

P.B. slid the stock of the Enfield against the stubble of his cheek. He heard it rasp slightly then felt the hairs bend softly.

As always, he felt projected along the barrel of the weapon, thrown towards the sight and through it out to the chosen target.

Leaves shivered around him. Insects droned. He could hear Deacon snapping at Shan but he could not make out the words. Shan shambled coolie-fashion, the butcher boy reverting to type.

Distance, corporal?

Four hundred and forty yards, sir.

When Shan lifted his head, the lens of his glasses caught the sun, formed a bright half-penny spot upon which the Scot drew a fine and final bead.

P.B. emptied his lungs and, casually it seemed, fired.

Shot cleanly through the eye-socket, Wei Sand Shan fell dead.

P.B. sighed. It would be his last kill. He was done with the trade now, once and for all. He would pull out of the service as soon as Beasley could arrange it, hand back his bloody shilling to the King. It was the first round he had ever fired at an unarmed man and it would be the last. He had done it without regret, though, in defence of rightness and on principle.

Though he might fire no more, others would have to.

In the forest the locusts were, for a time, quite still.

'McNair? McNair? You damned fool,' Deacon shouted from the pathway below. 'Why did you do it?'

'Because *you* wouldn't,' P.B. cried. 'Because *you* bloody wouldn't,' and swung down from the oak tree to the ground.

James Albany

SAS 1: Warrior Caste £1.25

Book 1 in the fighting saga of the SAS. France 1940 – as the Panzers pursued their thrust to the sea, a crack SS unit came to the small town of St Felice, in search of a very special English fugitive. Their orders from the Fuhrer were to take the Englishman whatever the cost. But other men were coming to St Felice – Lieutenant Deacon and the burly Canadian Buz Campbell, with a secret weapon that the SS couldn't match: Corporal McNair. Their job – to find the mysterious Englishman and bring him back alive.

James Barwick

The Hangman's Crusade £1.75

SS General Reinhard Heydrich. In ten years he had risen from a clerk in the newborn Nazi party to Reichsprotektor of Czechoslovakia. The Czechs called him 'The Hangman'. On 27 May, 1942, under orders from London, they shot him down on the streets of Prague ...

Why was he of all the Nazi gangsters singled out for assassination? Why did London order his death when they knew that Nazi vengeance would cost tens of thousands of Czech lives?

Alexander Fullerton

All the Drowning Seas £1.50

February 1942: as Japan's war machine sweeps across the Pacific, a handful of warships prepare for the last-ditch defence of Java. In command of the cruiser *Defiant*, a badly wounded Nick Everard knows defeat is inevitable. Two ships and two ships' companies can choose only between captivity and death ...

'For research, detail and inside knowledge of the soul of a fighting ship, Fullerton is the admiral of the moderns' OBSERVER

Heinz G. Konsalik

Strike Force 10 £1.75

The exhausted Wehrmacht battalions are awaiting a new Soviet offensive on the Eastern Front and the Allies are sweeping inexorably across Europe to deal the death blow to Germany itself. As crushing defeat looks inevitable the masters of Nazi Germany summon ten officers to a briefing in Berlin. Their destination is Russia. There they are to kill Stalin.

Guy Wheeler

Cato's War £1.50

Cato's war was the blood and terror duel between George Washington's rebels and Cornwallis's mercenaries, fought with sparse honour and no quarter, across colonies that history had seized by the throat . . .

'A clear and lively picture of important events seen from an unusual angle . . . a vivid narrative . . . well-researched and well told' GENERAL SIR JOHN HACKETT, THE TIMES

Peter Fox

Mantis £1.50

Mantis is a guided cruise missile developed by the British. Suddenly scientists connected with the project are eliminated. Somebody is after the plans. There is a nameless man in the background, pulling the strings. There is a strong indication that Israel may be the villain . . .

'Unusually deft . . . brilliantly organized . . . superbly written' NEW YORK TIMES

Wilbur Smith
The Eye of the Tiger £1.75

'A blood-and-cyclone story . . . action follows action, menace mingles with violence and horror and Harry Fletcher with blonde and brunette . . . Mystery is piled on mystery . . . death on brutal death as Fletcher hunts the Mozambique Channel for the ocean's unknown treasure. A tale to delight the millions of addicts of the gutsy adventure story' SUNDAY EXPRESS

Cry Wolf £1.95

Two men, one girl and a batch of decrepit armoured cars running the gauntlet of an Ethiopia in the grip of the Wolf of Rome – 'Mussolini has all the guns, aircraft and armour he needs. The jolly old Ethiop has a few ancient rifles and a lot of two-handed swords . . . It should be a close match!'

'Another cracker . . . Africa, arms dealing, armoured cars, strong men with stronger women all combine beautifully for real entertainment' DAILY MIRROR

Eagle in the Sky £1.75

In Israel's nerve-stretching struggle for survival, David Morgan's brilliance as a Mirage pilot is his passport to Debra's love. But terrorism and tragedy spawned by the violence that drew them together threaten to tear them apart. From savage air-fights over the desert to hand-to-hand conflicts on a South African game reserve, this unforgettable story blends intense excitement with a tender, sensual love . . .

Mario Puzo
The Godfather £1.95

'A staggering triumph . . . the definitive novel about a sinister fraternity of crime' SATURDAY REVIEW

'A splendid and distinguished blood saga of the Cosa Nostra, the American Mafia, and of the whirl created by five families of *mafiosi* at war in New York' SUNDAY TIMES

Robin Cook
Sphinx £1.25

Beautiful Egyptologist Erica Baron is mesmerized by a centuries-old statue in a Cairo antique shop, believing she has found the key to a dazzling hoard of untapped treasure. But there are others, more ruthless and corrupt than herself, determined to get there first, whatever the cost. Lost in a deadly web of intrigue and murder, Erica races to unlock the secrets of a pharaoh's tomb and plumb the curse that has kept it intact since time began . . .

Garson Kanin
Moviola £1.50

The Hollywood novel that tells it all.

Meet 92-year-old B. J. Farber, rich and cantankerous, a movie mogul about to sell his legendary studios. This is his story – the scandals, heartbreaks, passions and mysteries – Fatty Arbuckle's sex disgrace, Chaplin the comic genius, Garbo's tragic romance, the discovery of Monroe and her mysterious death, the trials and backroom feuds behind some of the greatest films ever made.

'More film stars' real secrets than there are footprints in the cement of Hollywood Boulevard' DAILY MAIL

Alexander Fullerton
Last Lift from Crete £1.50

May 1941. Out of the Cretan skies came the savage onslaught of the Stukas . . . The Royal Navy was to carry the heat and the burden of the evacuation of Crete, running the gauntlet of the Luftwaffe. For Nick Everard, commanding the destroyer *Tuareg*, it meant lifting stranded troops and a field hospital from the wrong side of Crete, where dawn would find his ships still within stalking distance of the murderous Stukas.

Leonard St Clair
Obsessions £1.50

The seventeenth of July was to be a glittering day for European and American high society: the wedding of Orsino di Ascoli, multi-millionaire at the head of a titanic business empire, and Erin Deering, star of the cinema screen.

From the shadows, others are watching; among them Lisa di Ascoli, the seductive heiress with the heart of ice. The shadows are filled with hate and vengeance. The shadows reach back over four decades to the hour when priceless gems were torn from the breast of a dead Tsarina as Bolshevik bullets cut down the Imperial Romanovs in Ekaterinburg on the seventeenth of July . . .

Leslie Thomas
That Old Gang of Mine £1.50

Meet ODDS – the Ocean Drive Delinquent Society – a band of geriatric drop-outs chasing excitement and danger in their twilight years in the Florida sun. There's Ari the Greek, K-K-K-K-Katy the dancing queen, Molly Mandy who supplies the gang's arms cache (and one and only bullet), and ex-hood Sidewalk Joe.

Hot on their heels comes the baffled Salvatore, local police captain, and bumbling private eye Zaharran. Never was organized crime so disorganized.

'Hilarious' DAILY MIRROR

☐	**The Diary of Anne Frank**	Anne Frank	£1.50p
☐	**Linda Goodman's Sun Signs**	Linda Goodman	£2.50p
☐	**Mountbatten**	Richard Hough	£2.50p
☐	**How to be a Gifted Parent**	David Lewis	£1.95p
☐	**Symptoms**	Sigmund Stephen Miller	£2.50p
☐	**Book of Worries**	Robert Morley	£1.50p
☐	**The Hangover Handbook**	David Outerbridge	£1.25p
☐	**The Alternative Holiday Catalogue**	edited by Harriet Peacock	£1.95p
☐	**The Pan Book of Card Games**	Hubert Phillips	£1.75p
☐	**Food for All the Family**	Magnus Pyke	£1.50p
☐	**Everything Your Doctor Would Tell You If He Had the Time**	Claire Rayner	£4.95p
☐	**Just Off for the Weekend**	John Slater	£2.50p
☐	**An Unfinished History of the World**	Hugh Thomas	£3.95p
☐	**The Third Wave**	Alvin Toffler	£1.95p
☐	**The Flier's Handbook**		£5.95p

All these books are available at your local bookshop or newsagent, or can be ordered direct from the publisher. Indicate the number of copies required and fill in the form below 7

Name ______________________________
(Block letters please)

Address ______________________________

____

Send to Pan Books (CS Department), Cavaye Place, London SW10 9PG
Please enclose remittance to the value of the cover price plus:
35p for the first book plus 15p per copy for each additional book ordered to a maximum charge of £1.25 to cover postage and packing
Applicable only in the UK

While every effort is made to keep prices low, it is sometimes necessary to increase prices at short notice. Pan Books reserve the right to show on covers and charge new retail prices which may differ from those advertised in the text or elsewhere